Praise for Marvin Albert's Stone Angel Series

THE LAST SMILE

"In a rapid-paced, alluring story of double-dealings, forgeries and assassinations, Albert utilizes the backdrops of Paris and Venice to their best advantage."

Publishers Weekly

LONG TEETH

"A smoothly written exercise in detection. The story is told in a straightforward manner, but Albert spices it up by putting in numerous plot twists and turns."

Rave Reviews

STONE ANGEL

"The narrative moves quickly, the characters are human and likable, and Albert is adept at conveying contemporary French society."

Publishers Weekly

THE MIDNIGHT SISTER

Marvin Albert

FAWCETT GOLD MEDAL • NEW YORK

A Fawcett Gold Medal Book
Published by Ballantine Books
Copyright © 1989 by Marvin Albert

Library of Congress Catalog Card Number: 88-92926

ISBN 0-449-13163-7

Manufactured in the United States of America

First Edition: June 1989

for Xenia
with love and kisses
from Pete Sawyer

𒊹 **1** 𒊹

THE PRINCIPALITY OF MONACO IS THE LAST PLACE ALONG the Côte d'Azur that a rational hit man would choose to kill or otherwise savage an intended victim. It is too small, with too few ways to get out of it in a hurry. And it has more cops and more surveillance TV cameras per square inch than any sovereign country I know—even the few others of similar vest-pocket size.

So I didn't burn rubber getting there. But I didn't dawdle either. Arlette Alfani was not a nervous type. And she was used to attracting attention from men she didn't know. When a woman looks like Arlette, she's bound to get used to it. If she sensed something disturbing about the man she spotted tailing her around Monaco, it was unlikely to be her imagination overworking.

Arlette did have a rich fantasy life. But in my experience— and I'd known her for some eleven years, since she was seventeen—her fantasies were as specialized as they were stimulating, bubbling to the surface only while making love. She was not subject to the sort that stir unwarranted fears.

Her childhood had taught her to differentiate between real and imagined dangers. For some decades before his retirement her father had been one of the heavy-leverage gangsters on the south coast of France—frequently at war with his competitors. One of Marcel Alfani's brothers, Arlette's Uncle

1

Emile, was killed by a long-range rifle while walking across the lawn of her home. She was eight at the time, and she got a good look at what a bullet can do to a man's face when she ran outside before Marcel Alfani could grab and stop her.

When she was eleven, another of her uncles, Bartolemy, got transmuted into bloody hamburger by a car bomb just after dropping her off at school. The force of the blast carried far enough to throw her ten feet across the schoolyard.

Two years later there was a machine gun attack on a small restaurant where her daddy was treating her to dinner. Alfani still had the necessary instant reflexes back then, and he'd dumped his daughter to the floor and thrown himself on top of her the instant the first burst smashed through the front window. Neither was hit. But another diner near them was killed, and three others severely wounded by the prolonged barrage.

Growing up bombarded by experiences like that could traumatize you for life unless you'd built yourself, while still very young, a solid layer of protective cool. The only sign of possible trauma I'd ever detected about Arlette was her decision to become an attorney and devote her near-genius IQ to both law and justice. (That those two were not always the same was something else she'd grasped early on.) Her cool was formidable. She did have that fiery Corsican temper that sometimes burned through the cool in spite of her best efforts to keep it banked. But never an irrational attack of the jitters.

So I didn't dawdle on my way to her.

It was a bright Sunday morning in March. Balmy. With a light blue sky and a dark blue Mediterranean meeting far out along a horizon line so sharply defined you could have cut paper on it. We'd had the soft winter and early spring that first-time visitors to the Riviera always expect and sometimes actually get. With the mimosas and almond trees and irises in full bloom at the beginning of February. March was following through nicely.

The sun this morning was already strong enough for the

beaches to be dotted with sunbathers and for some of them to be taking their first dip of the day. I'd been down to the little cove below my house earlier for my own wake-up swim. Half an hour straight out to sea, half an hour back. Climbing back up the steep wooded slope to the house feeling nicely loose, clearheaded, and hungry. Hungry enough to devour a full American-style breakfast. A heaping plateful of eggs with bacon and toast. Followed by a hefty slice of delicious *tarte aux pommes* with my second cup of coffee.

Then I'd taken my shower and gotten dressed for a couple hours of tackling house repairs. Faded jeans and an aging blue denim shirt. I'd been shoving my bare feet into a pair of tennis sneakers when the phone call came through from Arlette in Monaco.

Another thing Arlette got from her peculiar childhood was a nose for professional hard cases. That was what she smelled about the guy following her: hoodlum.

"He's been in prison," she told me. "More than once, and he's not the type to be too upset by it. Right at home with the other habituals."

It took me less than ten minutes to drive from my house to the place where she was waiting: the morning market in the Condamine section of Monaco. Behind the curve of the old port. Between the hill crowned by the palace and the other hill that just manages to support the massed architectural weight of the principality's overbuilt Monte Carlo section.

Most of the big square fronting the covered and open Condamine food markets was crammed with the parked cars and vans of shoppers and vendors. I eased my Peugeot 205 into a narrow slot between a Jeep and a Mercedes sedan. That put me behind a sleek red Maserati Biturbo that was blocking the rear of a Mitsubishi pickup nosed against the curb.

Like everybody else parked there, I left the keys in my ignition. If the drivers of the vehicles trapped in front of mine wanted out while I was away, they could shift my car. If they were newcomers shy about doing so, one of the splendidly uniformed cops watching the square would usually stroll over and lend a hand.

It's the only way the sellers of fruit and vegetables, seafood and flowers, can circulate enough customers to pocket a profit. That profit, it is true, has become small change in relation to the tiny country's gambling and real estate affluence. All the food stands together don't clear as much in a week as any single table over at the casinos can rake in in an hour. But the market has been part of the Monaco scene longer than its high rises and high rollers. The prince likes to make sure a few of the old traditions don't go under. During market hours the Monegasque hucksters have more clout than even the billionaire resident foreigners who use the principality as their tax shelter.

I zigzagged between the parked cars and crowds surrounding the outdoor food stands under their big square shade umbrellas. The air smelled of citrus fruit and roses and fish. Arlette sat at one of the tables in the arcade outside the Eden Bar, wearing a blue silk scarf with a white blouse and tailored blue slacks. She was taking a lusty bite out of a rich pastry as I approached. My guess was she'd finished off another like it while waiting. Arlette's appetite was as vigorous as everything else about her, and she was still young enough to get away with it.

Her raven-black hair, cropped short in a fruitless attempt to make herself look more like a serious professional woman and less of a femme fatale, gleamed in a shaft of sunlight piercing the foilage of a nearby plane tree. Her eyes, almost as dark as her hair, narrowed just a bit when she saw me coming her way. She betrayed no other sign of recognition. Taking a sip of coffee, she leaned back in her chair and gazed above and beyond me, at the oldest section of the Monaco castle looming above the square, its ramparts festooned with small pines and palms.

Her overnight bag was on the terrace beside her, together with a plastic sack filled with groceries. She had taken the night train to Milan on Friday to be part of an Italian TV program about how European women were faring in business and the other professions. The women sharing the discussion panel with her consisted of two Italians, a Swede, a German, and a Spaniard. Arlette had been invited to represent France because, like many Corsicans, she spoke Italian as fluently as French. After the program, and a dinner party laid on by the television station, she'd taken the Saturday night train back.

She had first seen the man among the people waiting on the platform when she got off the train in Monaco this morning. Her car was in a parking garage near the Condamine market, a short walk from the station. Arlette had stopped first at the market, to buy food for us. We'd made a date to have lunch together at my place this Sunday. That was why she'd taken the train from Monaco, instead of Nice, where she lived.

She'd noticed the same man again while she was buying shrimps and oysters at an outdoor stand. After spotting him again while she was inside the covered market making other purchases, Arlette had become pretty sure he was tailing her. To make double sure, she'd taken a stroll around the block behind the market. A stop to look at a display in a clothing store window had given her his reflection: a quarter of a block behind her.

It didn't scare her. But she did want to know who he was and why he was following her. What she wanted from me was help to insure that the answers she got were true.

It was impossible for me to spot any one man around the food stands or at another table paying special attention to Arlette. Much of the male population within range was doing that. A man who wasn't distracted by a woman with Arlette's face and figure needed antifreeze pumped into his veins. When I reached her table, I slowed my pace and turned my head for a long look at her in passing. It would have been conspicuous if I hadn't.

There was some powdered sugar on her ripe lower lip. The impulse to bend down and lick it off was powerful. Maybe powerful enough to reach her telepathically. The tip of her tongue flicked out and beat me to it. Then she picked up the last of her pastry and gave that her full attention. I walked on into the Eden.

The bar and tables were full up and standing room between them was packed. Most of the customers were having back-up breakfasts: coffee and croissants. There was also the usual minority getting the morning drinking well under way. Beer, white wine, pastis. The long, narrow room was hazy with pungent cigarette smoke.

The guy who owned the place was serving at the far end of the bar. His assistant, Jason Tripp, was working his way through the standing crowd in my direction with a smooth-flowing agility that was beautiful to watch. His loaded tray was balanced effortlessly on one huge hand held ear high. He was setting down orders and scooping up empties with barely a pause at each table. Swift elegance in motion. A perfect transfer of learned skills from one profession to an entirely different one.

Jason Tripp was a bronze-skinned black man from Detroit. Thirty years old and six feet eight inches tall. Ever since Europe had caught basketball fever its team recruiters had been scouting the States for experienced quality players. It was six years ago that a scout from the Monaco team had made Jason a heavy offer. By then Jason had become a pretty good pro but knew he wasn't going to get better enough to become a headliner. Not in the States. In Europe, against less hotshot competition, he had become one of the best.

It was a brief glory. One year. Then he began having trouble with his heart. Tachycardia. Not a dangerous condition, the doctors explained, if you were careful to avoid too much tension and exertion. That ended Jason's basketball career, and after his one-year taste of life on the Côte d'Azur he had no desire to go back where he'd come from. So he became a barman, settled in, and married a Monegasque: a nurse at the Princess Grace Hospital. Her being a citizen of Monaco—a privilege restricted to less than six thousand people with several generations of grandparents born there—gave them first dibs on Monaco's severely limited low-cost apartments. Between that and their two salaries, they lived very pleasantly.

Unlike me, Jason *never* got homesick for America.

He smiled when he saw me. A warm, relaxed smile, nothing held back. That was another reason Jason would never go home. Back there he was black and I was white. Over here we were both just American expatriates.

"Hey, Pete—guess you saw the Corsican bomber out there."

"She's kinda hard to overlook."

"For sure. That's one totally yummy girlfriend you got yourself. Better nail her down soon, before she—"

"You've got to be elderly, female, and Jewish to get into the matchmakers' union, Jason. Did you see this guy who's been following her?"

Jason nodded. "Let me get shut of this tray." He went around the near end of the bar. I leaned my elbows on it and waited. Arlette had told him what was going on before using the Eden's phone booth to call me. He came back with a towel and used it to wipe the bar, bringing his head down inches from mine.

I said, "Where's the guy now?"

"Don't know. He went into the covered market right after Arlette sat down outside; ain't spotted him since."

"What's he look like?"

"Almost as big as you. Maybe almost as mean, too. That kind of mouth. Yellow hair, going bald. Wraparound sunglasses, checked sport jacket, black slacks."

One of the early drinkers, a heavy man with a network of

broken blood vessels decorating his cheeks, came up beside us with an empty beer glass and asked Jason for a refill. Jason put a big paw against the man's shoulder and gently but firmly pushed him away, the full length of his extralong arm. ''Hold on to your thirst a minute,'' he told him in perfect French, and then looked back to me and said in rapid English: ''Any way I can help?''

''When Arlette comes in to pay her bill,'' I said, ''tell her to grab a cab at the train station and have it take her over to Monte Carlo, then circle back and out to my place by way of the lower corniche.''

Jason nodded. ''Think this guy trailing her's real trouble?''

''That's what I'm about to find out,'' I said, and went back outside.

2

I STROLLED PAST ARLETTE TO THE PLACE WHERE THE TWO right-angled market arcades met. From there I had a view of the entire square. While I watched and waited I struck up a casual conversation with one of the hucksters I knew: Veronique Leone, an attractive, gentle-eyed woman in her forties who liked working the morning market because it left the rest of the day for her reading. Veronique took more books out of her local library in any two weeks than most people read in a year.

She was telling me about her latest—a collection of Joseph Brodsky's poetry—when Arlette got up from her table. I watched her dig a purse out of her shopping sack and go inside the Eden Bar to pay what she owed.

A moment later the guy Jason Tripp had described made his appearance. He stepped out from behind the news kiosk in the center of the square, crossed the traffic lane, and came through the tangle of parked cars toward the Eden.

He was about six feet tall, thickset, with heavy shoulders and a wide, hard-muscled jaw. In his late thirties. The receding hair *was* yellow, like Jason had said, not blond. A bad dye job. When he got closer, I saw what Jason meant about that mouth. It had a viciously tight look, as though his lips were stretched by a permanent facial cramp.

I saw, too, what Arlette had registered about him.

The kind of habitual criminals for whom serving prison time is an expected part of normal life come in all varieties. But they share certain traits picked up inside the walls. This one had them. The deadpan watchful expression, emphasized rather than hidden by the masklike sunglasses. The stoic patience about the way he moved: like he was still doing exercise turns around a jailyard, keeping to himself but ready for sudden violence from any direction.

But I don't think I would have pegged him for a hood as immediately as Arlette had, if she hadn't given me her own feeling beforehand.

I'd dealt with more than my share of underworld characters. First as a Chicago cop, and then as an investigator in Europe for the federal narcs and a Senate committee, before going private. But childhood experiences merge knowledge into an instinct more dependable than anything an adult can acquire. Compared to Arlette's childhood, mine had been a period of utter innocence. Summer on the Côte d'Azur with my French mother. School terms in Chicago with the protective parents of my American father who'd died four months before I was born.

The fact that my grandfather had been a Chicago police captain hadn't given me any insight at all into the criminal world. He was always careful to keep his work strictly separated from his family. Which probably accounted for my growing up with the impression that his profession was a mysteriously fascinating one I wanted to get into. Not the smartest decision I'd ever made, it often occurred to me later. Too late to go another route . . .

Veronique Leone was telling me that what impressed her most about Brodsky's poems was their simple style and down-to-earth subject matter.

The hood I was watching took up a position against an arcade column near the Eden Bar.

I told Veronique I wondered how close the French translator had come to the sound and feeling of Brodsky's Russian.

Arlette emerged from the bar. The hood sidestepped out of sight behind the column.

Veronique was replying to my question when she interrupted herself in midsentence and said quietly: ''You're working, aren't you?'' Her gentle eyes didn't miss much.

I nodded. Arlette had picked up her shopping sack and overnight bag and was walking away. She turned into Avenue Prince Pierre, the short street that sloped up to the Monaco railroad station. The hood reappeared and strolled after her.

Veronique Leone turned to wait on a couple customers. I went around the end of her food stand and tailed the hood.

There was enough pedestrian traffic so I could stick close to him without being noticed. I didn't try to get close enough to make a fast grab. If he hadn't made a move on Arlette in all the time since he'd begun following her, he wasn't going to. At least not here in Monaco. Which wasn't the best place for me to start trouble either. Not if my objective was to help Arlette get straight answers out of him.

It was between train arrivals at the station. There were four taxis outside waiting for the next one. Arlette got into the first taxi. As it started up, the hood climbed into the second in line. Arlette's pulled away from the station and the hood's taxi followed it.

They were angling toward Boulevard Prince Albert I, which led along the port to the Monte Carlo section. Arlette would most likely go around the seaside of Monte Carlo via Boulevard Louis II. After that she could use either Avenue Princess Alice or Boulevard Prince Ranier III to circle back. While they were negotiating all that royalty I had time to get myself in position.

I went back down to the market. My Peugeot had been shifted to a different slot while I was gone. There was a four-door Fiat Uno blocking it now. Getting the Peugeot out required four separate operations. I had to back the Fiat into the traffic lane, then back out my car, return the Fiat to its slot, and finally get in my car and drive off.

I swung around to the lower corniche where it cut west in the direction of my house. As soon as Monaco was behind me, and I was back on French soil, I pulled off the side of the road. Putting the car in neutral and leaving the motor running, I dug my emergency pistol out of its hidden compartment inside the backseat. I hadn't been reckless enough to chance carrying it around on me inside Monaco. I didn't think the hood trailing Arlette would be that dumb either—which would mean he wasn't armed now. But I couldn't be totally sure of that.

My car gun was a compact Heckler & Koch P7. Leaving its holster in its hiding place, I laid the pistol on the front seat beside me, close to hand. I covered it with a Levi's jacket I'd brought along when I'd left the house. Then I wound both front windows all the way open, and waited.

Arlette cruised by in her taxi six minutes later. The hood's taxi went past me a second after that. I pulled back onto the road and followed.

We went through Cap d'Ail, the nearest village to my house, and continued on beyond it—with the last cliffs of the Maritime Alps looming above the right side of the road and dropping away from the left side into the sea. After we had negotiated two short tunnels through the cliffs, the gate of the driveway leading down to my house appeared on the left. The first taxi swung over and stopped outside the gate. Arlette got out and began paying the driver.

The second taxi kept going, passing her and disappearing around a sharp bend in the cliff on the right. I slowed the Peugeot as I went after it.

Beyond the bulge of the cliff the taxi had stopped beside the road and the hood was climbing out. I drove past and turned into the Fina gas station a few yards farther on. Behind me the taxi made a U-turn and sped back toward Monaco. The hood began walking alongside the road in the same direction, moving fast now. When he was out of sight around the bend I drove out of the Fina station and turned back.

By the time I reached the other side of the bend both taxis were gone. Arlette was inside the gate now. It was always kept locked so nobody could drive in except those who had keys to it: the small number like me, with houses along the driveway that hairpinned down the steep slope on the other side. But anyone could walk in. There was a narrow curved passage for people on foot to get around the gate. That was what Arlette had used. Her overnight bag and shopping sack were on the ground. She stood looking through the bars of the gate, openly observing the hood's approach on the other side of the road.

His hands were still empty. I slowed to a crawl and watched him cross the road toward Arlette. When he was almost there I accelerated, spun the car between him and the gate, and braked to a skidding halt after missing him by inches. He leaped backward, momentarily startled out of his jailhouse phlegm. Then he froze in position, spreading his hands out to either side of him as he looked into the mouth of the gun I held aimed at him through the car window.

"What is this?" he bleated. "I ain't done anything."

He didn't sound as tough as he looked.

"Hands on your head," I snapped. "Turn around with your back to me."

He obeyed both instructions instantly, automatically. When you've been a cop, some of it clings to you, in spite of your best efforts. At least enough of it for someone of this guy's considerable experience to see and hear. Sometimes it helps.

I got out of the car and stepped to one side: "Now, hands on top of the car."

He turned and obeyed that order automatically, too. Without having to be told, he spread his feet and slid them backward until his braced hands were taking much of his leaning weight. He'd been through the routine often enough to have it down pat.

"Just tell me what I did wrong," he said in a bored tone while I patted him down. He had his stoic apathy back in working order. "Did I bust some law I don't know about?"

He wasn't carrying any kind of weapon. I took his wallet and had a look at his ID. "Jean-Philippe Roux," I read aloud. "Your real name?"

"So my mamma always told me."

I looked at Arlette, who had come around to our side of the gate. "Mean anything to you?"

"No."

According to his ID he lived in Lyons. "This address," I asked him, "that real, too?"

"My girlfriend's place. Used to stay there, sometimes, before I went up for my last stretch. Don't know if she'll be interested in having me back. I came straight down here after I got out."

I took off his sunglasses and looked to Arlette again. She shook her head. She still didn't know him. I told him to sit on the ground and place his hands on his raised knees. That way he couldn't make any sudden move fast enough to catch me off guard. Also in that position my car hid him, along with the gun I was holding on him, from people in any cars that passed along the road.

Roux—if that was really his name—settled down where I pointed, keeping his bored expression in place. He looked up at Arlette and said, "I only wanted to talk to you a minute. Just talk is all; nothing to get this worked up about."

"Are you shy?" Arlette demanded.

He said, "Huh?"

"You've been following me around ever since I got off the train. Does it usually take you this long to get up the nerve to talk to a woman?"

"I didn't know if you might get scared or something," Roux explained. "Maybe start yelling for the cops. Those cops in Monaco—they don't like people like me on their turf. People that've done time. So I was waiting till you got out've there.'' He looked sourly from Arlette to me. ''Seems like you called the cops anyway.''

''He's not a cop.''

Roux nodded sagely. ''Sure.'' He didn't sound entirely convinced.

''Used to be,'' I told him. ''Not anymore.''

''Okay,'' Roux said, dead flat.

''Now that you're here and I'm here,'' Arlette said to him, ''what did you want to talk to me about? You need an attorney?''

''Not me. It's . . .'' Roux hesitated, looking at me again.

''I *told* you he's not a cop,'' Arlette growled.

Arlette can whomp up a growl that shocks hell out of people, coming from someone who looks like her.

Roux blinked. Then he thought it over for a couple more seconds. Finally he shrugged. ''What the hell,'' he said, half to himself.

We waited for him to say something that made sense to us.

He took a breath and told Arlette, ''Dédé Colin wants to see you.''

Something cold brushed lightly across the back of my neck.

French peasants say that means a devil passing by.

# 3

HIS REAL NAME WAS ANDRÉ COLIN. BUT THE NEWS MEDIA had long ago taken to using his nickname—Dédé—and tacked an alliterative label onto it: *le Dingue*. Literally, the mad dog.

Dédé *le Dingue* or André Colin—either name could spread a momentary chill even among his fellow denizens of the European underworld. His first murder went back to when he was sixteen. Colin's hide-and-seek transit through the dozen years that followed had left a trail of armed robberies and unpredictable, passionless killings behind him. Culminating at a Riviera villa on Cap d'Antibes last year, when he'd pulled off the biggest gem haul in French history and added two more violent deaths to his record.

I saw the name jolt Arlette. She had represented him in court after he had finally been captured and brought to trial. There was only one way Colin could come out of it with a lesser sentence than he deserved, Arlette had told him. By offering to reveal the whereabouts of all that jewelry—not a single piece of which had turned up anywhere since the Antibes heist—in exchange for a deal with the government. Colin wouldn't go for it. So Arlette had tried her best with the only alternative—an insanity plea. There was enough basis for that. But the court hadn't bought it. Colin was now doing a life sentence in Fresnes Prison. With no possibility of parole.

Colin had blamed Arlette for that. He'd claimed she had deliberately fumbled his defense to help the government pressure him into that deal. And he had warned her that he'd get back at her for it someday, one way or another.

Arlette was having trouble swallowing that memory. I gave her some more time, asking Roux, "When did Colin ask you to get in touch with Mademoiselle Alfani?"

"Two days ago. Day before I got out of Fresnes. I was doing five for robbery. But they let me out yesterday after only half." Roux smiled a little. "Good behavior. Every indication I'm a reformed character."

"And the jails are too overcrowded to waste the space on small fry like you."

"There's that, too," Roux agreed blandly.

Arlette finally spoke up. "Why the rush about giving me Colin's message? You got out of prison yesterday and the first thing on your mind is finding me?"

Roux turned his head to look up at her. "Because that's what Dédé wanted me to do. So that's what I did. Phoned your apartment but your answering machine said you were off at this TV station in Milan. So I call there but they tell me you already left and they don't know where else you can be reached. But they do know you've got a ticket for a sleeping compartment on the night train back from Milan to Monaco. So that's where I waited for you. In case you didn't go back to your place today. On account of it's tomorrow he wants to see you."

"What does Colin want to talk to me about?" Arlette asked him.

"He said to tell you he's decided you were right after all. He's ready to make that deal you talked to him about. I don't know what deal he means and I don't want to know. If I don't know, I can't get in trouble for passing on the message. Right?" Roux turned his head to look at me again. "Can I get up now? My neck's starting to hurt from having to look up like this."

"Not yet," I told him. "You know Colin from before you went up?"

Roux shrugged. "We bumped into each other a couple times in bars is all. I knew who he was, naturally. But I don't think he even knew my name. I'm not a celebrity like him."

"But you got to know each other better after he joined you in Fresnes."

"We bumped into each other more, sure. Prison's a little world. But we never got to be pals, if that's what you mean. I wasn't a celebrity in prison either. And Dédé is. He'd talk to me, sometimes, like to anybody else, just to pass the time. About the food, the guards, this and that. Nothing personal."

"You must have gotten closer than that," I said. "For you to go to all this trouble for him. And for him to trust you to."

"What he trusts," Roux said flatly, "is that I know if I don't do what he wants and he ever gets out, he'll come after me and kill me."

"He say that?"

"A guy like Dédé Colin doesn't have to say it for you to know he'll do it."

True.

Arlette asked him, "That's all he told you to say to me?"

"Pretty much. Just he wants to talk to you. About some deal. And tomorrow—that's important. No later than tomorrow."

"Why?"

"That's something else I don't know," Roux said. "All he said was it's got to be Monday or forget it. If you don't come see him at Fresnes tomorrow, he'll work out the deal through some other lawyer."

"Nothing else?"

"That's all of it," Roux said.

Arlette looked at me with an abstracted frown. "Let him go."

I told Roux he could get up. He shoved to his feet and

moved his head around to get a crick out of his neck. When I gave him back his wallet and sunglasses, he asked me, "Can you drive me back to my car? It's in—"

"No," I told him. "Walk around that bend to the Fina station. You can phone for a taxi from there."

"Thanks," he said disgustedly. He put away his wallet and gave Arlette an admiring smile. "Well, it was nice meeting you."

He was starting to turn away when she stopped him with another question: "How is Colin taking prison? He's been in there almost seven months now. How does he look?"

"Like always," Roux told her. "Cheerful and scary."

We watched him put on his sunglasses and trudge off down the road.

◨ 4 ◨

I OPENED THE OYSTERS AND SHELLED THE SHRIMPS. GENerous helpings of both. I distributed them equally on Arlette's plate and my own. Opening the mayonnaise I'd taken from her shopping bag, I spooned it into a small bowl and added herbs. I sliced the brown bread she'd bought at the market and buttered each slice. I whistled while I worked. Stubborn good cheer is an optimist's only weapon. Our plan, made before Arlette left for Milan, was for a leisurely Sunday afternoon in the sack. But at the moment that pleasant prospect seemed a bit clouded.

After getting the bottle of chilled rosé from the fridge, I paused in the kitchen archway and looked again toward the brick terrace on the other side of my living room's opened glass doors. Arlette was still out there, standing beside the age-gnarled olive tree. Her back was to me. Beyond her spread a vast vista of the Mediterranean. She was gazing in that direction but I didn't think her mind was on the view.

Outlined against the pale sky, her hair looked like a helmet of shiny black steel. She had showered and changed into a white cotton dress. It was cinched at the waist by a red silk sash with long ends that hung against the lush curve of her right hip. Fabulous legs. The kind that took their sweet time rising all the way to that provocative derriere. She was standing exactly as she'd been the last two times I'd looked. One raised hand against the trunk of the olive tree, her head tilted slightly to one side, her other hand thrust deep into the pocket of her skirt.

I uncorked the bottle and set it on the tray with the rest of our lunch. Adding two wineglasses, I carried the tray out to the terrace and put it down on the wicker table. Arlette still had her back to me. I settled into my chair and clinked a glass against the rosé bottle. It rang like a tiny bell.

Arlette swung around, startled. It took her several seconds to come all the way back from wherever her head had been. Then she smiled and came away from the olive tree toward me. Every step was a pleasure to watch. She hadn't put on anything under that dress. Which was unfair, if that message from Fresnes had put a crimp in our plans for this day.

She sat down across from me, rested her elbows on the table, and cupped her chin in her hands. "What I keep wondering about," she said, "is *why* Colin has had this sudden change of mind."

"He wants out," I said. "I don't care how cheerful and scary he still looks; nobody could enjoy the notion of spending the rest of his life in the joint."

"But even if I can work out that deal for him, the best we could hope for is a *chance* of parole in perhaps twenty years."

"Twenty years is better than life."

Arlette straightened and shook her head. "Not for someone like André Colin. You don't know him the way I do."

"I know he's as clever as he is crazy," I said while I filled our wineglasses. "Suppose Colin says the Antibes jewels are buried in a forest. Or some other type of confusing terrain. He can't draw a map that'll lead the cops to the exact spot. They have to take him to the area so he can look around and find it. And a bunch of his playmates are waiting there with guns to bust him loose. It's been done before."

"That's one of the things I don't like about this," Arlette said. "The possibility he's trying to use me to pull something."

"If you don't like it, don't go."

"You know I've already phoned in my plane reservation."

"Air France won't go broke if you cancel."

"What I don't want to cancel is a golden opportunity." Arlette gave me a wry smile. "*If* Colin means it—if *I* can be instrumental in recovering that fortune in jewelry—I'll feel like the worst fool on earth if I let some other attorney grab that away from me."

"Be a feather in your cap," I acknowledged.

"I can use it."

It galled Arlette that much of her career so far had been spent, not in court, but in the Nice offices of her law firm preparing cases for its senior partners, Henri and Joelle Bonnet. She was better than them at that; and not as successful as either in actually trying cases. What aggravated that was the fact that the Bonnets tended to let her hone her courtroom skills only on insignificant cases—or ones that were lost causes, like Colin's. But Arlette blamed most of her problem on her appearance. She claimed to be looking forward to midlife wrinkles and fat so judges would start listening to what she said in court, instead of just looking at her.

I handed her one of the wineglasses. "Simple choice. Go and listen to what Colin has to say. Or don't go, and forget it. Seems to me you've already decided."

"Yes." Arlette took a small sip of her rosé. "I'm going."

"Then quit batting it back and forth. Your plane isn't until tomorrow morning." I gestured at the oysters and shrimps. "And these are reputed to be chock-full of potent stimulants for the libido. If you're going to spend the time between now and morning brooding about that jailbird, we'd better go out and eat something else."

Arlette regarded me speculatively for a long moment. She took a longer sip of wine and put the glass down. Then she carefully selected a particularly large shrimp, dipped it into the mayonnaise bowl, and ate it, not taking her eyes off mine. Licking a dab of mayonnaise off her thumb, she said without change of expression, "Eat hearty, *mon vieux*. You're going to need all the libido you can manage."

She phoned me the next afternoon to tell me about her meeting in Fresnes Prison with André Colin.

"He says all of those jewels are still hidden together in one place and that he's the only one who knows where. He wants me to find out what the best deal is that the government will offer him before he says anything else."

"He explain why he's changed his mind about that?"

"Just that he'd prefer not to spend his old age as a convict."

"Think he's leveling with you?"

"Who knows what's going on inside that head of his? You can't tell anything from the way he looks or acts. As Roux said, still cheerful and scary. If Colin is tormented by prison life, it doesn't show."

"Where are you calling from?" I asked her.

"Paris," Arlette told me. "I have an appointment tomorrow at the Interior Ministry to discuss Colin's change of mind. And I'm seeing representatives of the insurance companies later today. I want them to apply pressure on the ministry to make the best offer possible within reason."

"Use my apartment while you're up there," I said. "You can get the key from Fritz."

"He already gave it to me. That's where I'm calling you from."

I had bought the apartment, next to Fritz Donhoff's in the Mouff quarter of Paris, back when we'd originally become partners. He still worked out of his, and our cases brought me to Paris often enough to make keeping mine worthwhile.

"How does Fritz look to you?" I asked Arlette.

"Better than when we saw him two weeks ago. But he's still not what he was before he was shot."

It was more than three months since a bastard Fritz was tailing put two bullets into him. Fritz had survived that thanks to an exceptionally strong constitution. But at seventy-four his recuperative powers weren't what they'd once been.

"Give him my love," I said.

"Sure. I already gave him mine."

"I take it he's healthy enough to enjoy that to the full."

"He's still a great kisser," Arlette informed me. "And he could teach you a few things about long, passionate hugs."

"Don't overdo it," I told her. "And keep me in touch with how this Colin business develops."

She promised that she would.

But it was from the TV news broadcast the following noon that I first learned what happened next.

André "Dédé" Colin had broken out of Fresnes that morning.

The police were investigating indications that Arlette had helped him escape.

☒ 5 ☒

THE FIRST IMAGE ON THE TELEVISION SCREEN WAS COLIN'S strong-boned face. A mug shot. He was grinning defiantly, his thick, neatly sculptured lips parted to show clenched teeth. Above that grin and the long, high-bridged nose, cold eyes stared dead-level into the camera lens. He looked more like an aristocrat than a thug. The kind of aristocrat who didn't share the same emotions as ordinary people. The kind that had brought on the French Revolution.

The news announcer's voice was quietly dramatic as she recounted the escape. It had been executed while prisoners from Fresnes's top-security wing, Colin among them, had been on their way to a morning exercise period. Colin had somehow slipped away from the others without being noticed. He had entered a prison administration building, using a side door normally locked from inside at all times. Nobody had so far explained how it had come to be unlocked this time.

The TV screen switched to an aerial view of the prison, with an arrow pointing to the building Colin had entered.

On his way up an inside stairway he'd encountered two guards. He had shot them both with a small revolver he was carrying, killing one and wounding the other. Then he'd raced to the top of the stairs and climbed a ladder to a trapdoor in the roof. As he emerged there a small helicopter flew in over the prison. While it hovered a couple feet above the roof, Colin scrambled onto one of its landing skids. There were two men inside the chopper's cabin: the pilot, and a passenger who fired an automatic rifle at the nearest guard tower to prevent the guards inside it from getting an accurate shot at Colin. He was still clinging to the chopper's skid when it lifted away from the prison and disappeared.

The TV screen switched again: to filmed footage of the helicopter—a little Alouette II—standing in a wheat field with uniformed cops around it. The police had found it abandoned there, a few miles from Fresnes. They had also found marks of a car's tires near it. But they hadn't found the car or Colin or the two men who'd been inside the chopper. Roadblocks had been set up all around the area, a nationwide search was on, and Interpol was alerting the rest of Europe. The authorities predicted that Colin and those who had aided in his escape would soon be in custody.

One question that remained unanswered, the announcer pointed out, concerned the unknown organization that had engineered it. The Alouette II had been rented from a nearby airport by two men ''for an hour's pleasure flight.'' Both men had been Oriental, but the pilot's license and other credentials presented by one of them said he was born in France. The police had already discovered these credentials to be false.

Another pertinent question: Who had told Colin exactly when to be on that prison roof, and given him the gun he'd used to get there? One possible explanation was currently being investigated by detectives questioning Colin's attorney. Her name was Arlette Alfani. She had been to the prison the previous day, for a meeting with Colin. They had met, as was customary, in the ''parlour''—a room allocated in every prison for private discussions between attorneys and their convict clients. As was also customary, what had transpired between Arlette Alfani and André Colin while in there together had been unobserved.

If, added the news announcer, the last name of Colin's attorney had a familiar sound, it was because her father was the notorious Marcel Alfani—now supposedly retired but for many years one of the most powerful gangsters in France.

It was not known, at this moment, if the police intended to question Marcel Alfani, as well as his daughter, concerning Colin's escape from the prison.

They were waiting for me in the living room of Fritz Donhoff's apartment in Paris. Fritz himself, Arlette, and the better half of the husband-wife team that ran her law firm, Joelle Bonnet.

I kissed Arlette and then held her shoulders for a moment and took a good look at her. "How did the cops treat you?"

"With polite suspicion," she said matter-of-factly. "My answers to their questions didn't seem to make them any less suspicious. Or less polite, for that matter. Don't worry, I'm not about to fall apart."

That was obvious. Her eyes, smile, and voice were steady as a rock. When the going gets tough . . .

Joelle Bonnet was sitting on Fritz's sofa, a plump woman in her mid-fifties with a placid face and a mind that could dazzle courtroom opponents into stuttering confusion. I kissed her on both cheeks. We'd known each other long enough for it to be more than a mannerly gesture.

Fritz stood up from his wing chair and we embraced. Over the years he'd come to be a sort of stand-in father for the real one I'd never known.

His full head of silvery hair had almost regained its former shine. The old-world charm was still intact. He held himself erect and was as elegantly dressed as always. But his big frame felt less bulky in my arms and his heavy-featured face hadn't regained its normal fleshiness either. Also, he was just a shade slower in standing up and sitting down again than he would have been before taking those two bullets.

I took a seat between Fritz and Arlette, facing Joelle across the coffee table. "What's the worst-situation analysis at this point?"

"The bottom line," Arlette said, "is that they suspect me of being the one who slipped Colin that gun and the timetable arranged for his escape. Naturally. I was the last one from outside to see him in prison before it happened. They have difficulty believing Colin asked me to come there just to dump me in this mess. His idea of a mean joke. To get even for what he considered my deliberate failure to get him a lesser sentence on an insanity plea. I can't blame them for not buying that. They know even less about how Colin's mind works than I do."

"What are they using as your motive?"

"I did it for a big share of whatever that stolen jewelry will bring," Arlette answered evenly. "At least they don't claim I'm in love with Colin. Maybe they will, after they think of that one."

"Your father's name doesn't help any."

She laughed softly. "No, not too much. Like father, like daughter. Or perhaps he planned the whole escape, to get his hands on the jewels, and I was only one of his tools. The police *have* thought of that one. They hinted about immunity for myself if I spill all about Papa."

"I had a talk with the *juge d'instruction* in charge of this case," Joelle said. "Immediately after arriving in Paris. At this point he's not making a formal charge against Arlette. Because, as he admits, he has no hard evidence to support it. What he has is *circumstantial* evidence pointing to her— and the lack of any evidence pointing to a more solid suspect. He won't be able to come up with real proof against Arlette in the future. Because she didn't do it. But Arlette *is* a suspect. And as such, of course, prohibited from practicing law from now on until this matter is cleared up."

"Which it may never be," Arlette said, looking at me. "Unless there are some investigators involved whose first interest is in my future. I've already given Fritz my check, retaining the two of you to work on that.''

''One hundred francs,'' Fritz told me, straight-faced.

That wouldn't pay our fee for one hour, let alone our expenses. The sole purpose of the check was to make us her legal representative in investigating the case.

''What did the *juge d'instruction* have to say about the ex-con who gave Arlette the message from Colin?'' I asked Joelle. ''Jean-Philippe Roux.''

''The police haven't been able to turn him up as yet. He doesn't seem to be in Lyons and his former girlfriend there says she hasn't heard from him.''

''I've already put out some preliminary feelers on Roux,'' Fritz told me.

The quantity and quality of his ''feelers'' were legendary. Over a career spanning more than fifty years—as a Munich police detective, an anti-Nazi assassin for the wartime Resistance, and a private investigator—Fritz had acquired a network of informants that the combined police forces of France probably couldn't match.

''But,'' he added, ''I am not too optimistic about the likelihood of Roux supporting Arlette's story when the police do find him.''

Arlette nodded agreement. ''As an ex-convict with a bad record he's much too vulnerable.''

I agreed, too. Passing unauthorized messages of any kind from a prisoner to the outside world was against the law. If Roux admitted he'd done that for a prisoner who escaped shortly afterward, he'd be sent up for another term—with his record probably for life.

Nobody had as yet bothered to point out that I could corroborate Arlette's story of the message Roux had given her. I would get around to doing so when I had time to spare, but there was no hurry. My relationship with Arlette made me someone with a personal reason to support her version—true or false. The police would receive my testimony the way they had hers, with polite doubt.

Joelle was looking worriedly from me to Fritz. "I don't know how you would go about learning who did give Colin that gun and tell him when the helicopter would be over that roof. But I get the impression the police aren't making any headway at all on that. Perhaps because their main efforts are presently concentrated elsewhere."

"Every prison has at least one guard open to a sizable bribe," Fritz said. "Usually more than one. They're underpaid and have the same needs as the rest of us. The answer to which one in Fresnes was paid to give Colin the gun comes with the answer to the larger and more important question: What criminal organization engineered the escape?"

Arlette stretched out her long legs and leaned back in her chair to ease her tension. She looked at me and kept her voice unemotional. "Colin is the one with all the answers."

I nodded. "We'll have to find him."

Joelle looked skeptical. "All the police of France are already trying to do that."

"Uh-huh," I said. "And if they find him, I'll give odds they won't be able to take him without killing him in the attempt. A dead Colin can't tell us what we need to know. We've got to get to him before they do."

"Can you?" Joelle demanded.

"That," Fritz told her quietly, "depends on our making the right choices about where to begin looking. Selecting a few points of departure. I suggest that we now put together everything we know about André Colin's past."

What we knew proved to be thin and disjointed. Even with Arlette contributing everything she'd learned during her pretrial conferences with Colin. But we did find a couple fragments in it that might reward deeper mining.

6

POVERTY, THAT CLASSIC BREEDER OF CRIME, HAD TO BE ruled out by those who later speculated about what had made André Colin go wrong. In the end they usually had to settle for the obvious: that he was born wrong. On that the psychologists and journalists seemed to be in rare agreement with the known facts.

Colin's father had been a plumber in the industrial city of Longwy, near the northern border of France. While he was far from rich, his income was up there with what most hard-working plumbers made anywhere. When André Colin was sixteen, his mother's uncle died in the Italian town of Treviso, leaving some property there to her and two Italian cousins. Deciding to cash in on Colin's mother's third of the property, Colin's parents traveled down to Treviso and took their son with them.

Negotiations with the two cousins dragged on. After several weeks of it Colin's mother, tired of haggling, was ready to settle for what the cousins offered. Colin's father wanted to hold out for more. There was an argument that got violent. Colin's father struck his wife, knocking her down.

Young André Colin walked away, came back with a hammer . . . and his father became the first victim to die by his hand.

Colin's mother testified that her husband had slapped her

around in the past, that her son couldn't stand it anymore, and had used the hammer only to protect her. The lawyer she hired pleaded temporary insanity provoked by the violence of the boy's father. The Italian authorities put André Colin into the Reggio Emilia mental hospital for an indeterminate period of intensive observation.

The preliminary diagnoses on Colin by the Reggio Emilia analysts, leaked to the media some years later, sounded as though they were exploring outer space. They found him "distant and cold, intelligent but difficult to reach." Deeper probes turned up "strong latent homicidal tendencies, unchecked by normal inhibitions." Colin was shifted to the hospital's prison wing. The examining psychiatrists warned that if he were ever released, he would almost certainly become a danger to society.

Colin was nineteen when he escaped, after using a broken glass to slash a guard's throat and taking his keys and gun.

The guard survived, but a young farm worker who caught Colin breaking into his car outside Verona that night didn't. When he drew a knife, Colin shot him, then took his identity papers in addition to his car. Before the young man died three hours later he described Colin to the police. By then Colin was far away. He drove into France, using the farm worker's papers, before wanted notices with his picture on them reached the frontier posts.

A week later Colin was identified—from pictures the French police had received from Italy—as the young man who'd held up a hunting equipment store in Aix-en-Provence, taking ammunition and two extra guns as well as the store's cash. After that Interpol began getting sporadic reports, from different parts of Europe, tentatively identifying Colin in further holdups. And two more killings.

It wasn't until almost five years after Colin's escape from Reggio Emilia that the French police got more definite information on him. From a captured bank robber named Gaetan Mora, who was part of a gang operating southeast of

Paris. In exchange for his liberty, Mora agreed to give the law the other four members of the gang. Including Colin, whom Mora fingered as the one responsible for the killing of a guard at a bank they'd hit in Dijon.

Mora didn't know much about Colin's background. Only what the chief of their gang had learned before recruiting Colin—from a fence in Paris: That he had been working as a loner, knocking over jewelry shops in France, Belgium, and Italy. And that he was handy with a gun. Not that Colin was a better shot than anybody else. It was just that he was always *ready* to shoot. He didn't need time to think it over first, and he didn't seem to worry about it after.

Evidence of that surfaced fairly soon after Colin joined the gang—in an argument with its leader. They'd just taken a bank near the Swiss border. Colin complained that the gang's chief was taking a larger share of the loot than any of the others. Their chief just opened his jacket and put his hand on the butt of his holstered pistol. Colin shrugged, said mildly that he was only asking, and turned away. Their chief grinned and dropped his hand. Colin turned back with a gun in his hand and shot him three times.

Then he announced he was taking over leadership of the gang.

The other four gang members had been armed at the time. But they didn't have their guns in hand and Colin did. They'd still been frozen by the sudden death of the man on the floor, and by the way Colin was smiling at them, when he sweetened his announcement. In the future loot would be shared equally between them, no extra cut for himself.

They had decided to give Colin a try. The results had given them no cause for complaint, other than never quite getting over being nervous around their new chief. Colin had proved to be smart at planning their jobs. And he'd kept his promise about taking no more of the loot than each of the others got.

One basic ingredient of criminality seemed to be lacking in Colin. He wasn't greedy.

"A strange one," Gaetan Mora told the cops. "Not exactly right in the head. You get a feeling he's in it for kicks, more than the dough. A *dingue*."

Gaetan Mora may have been the first one to call Colin a mad dog. He wasn't fated to enjoy that honor long.

Released from custody, Gaetan Mora led the cops to the other members of the gang. Three were taken without a fight. Colin was another matter.

It was a couple hours before dawn when they began surrounding the building where he was currently holed up. Either he had insomnia and spotted their preparations, or else he had a sixth sense when he slept. Colin went out a window into a back alley before the police trap was complete. He killed a cop who was entering the alley at that moment, broke into another building, and kept going.

The police spread their net wider, but Colin was gone. The hunt for him spread across France and into the other countries bordering it.

Three days later a Swiss frontier guard stopped a man driving over from France at the little village of Divonne-les-Bains. It was Colin, in a stolen car. The frontier guard suddenly spotted his resemblance to the wanted pictures and started to unholster his gun. The next instant he was down, gut shot, and Colin was sprinting into the forest that spreads across the Swiss-French border in that region. Within hours elite units from the Swiss and French police and army encircled the forest and began combing the interior, methodically searching every bush, tree, and cave.

They were still searching, two days later, when Gaetan Mora came out of a friend's place, far away to the southwest in Montpellier. He was going to his car when another one, driven by Colin, smashed into him. Then Colin stopped and backed up over the broken body to make doubly sure. He drove over what was left of Gaetan Mora a third time as he sped away.

He vanished after that. For more than a year. Not a single confirmed report on him came in to Interpol from any part of Europe. Not even an informer's tip on his possible whereabouts that stood up under investigation.

Until the night he hit that villa on Cap d'Antibes. Leading five other armed men who wore hoods that completely masked their faces. Colin did not. He never attempted to disguise himself when pulling a job. That appeared to be part of his macho image of himself. He liked having his exploits headlined by the media.

The villa on Cap d'Antibes belonged to a construction mogul. He was throwing a lavish costume party for his jet-set friends there that night. Since all his guests were as wealthy as himself, and as inclined to show it off, he had of course taken the precaution of hiring armed security men to protect the party. But after two of the security men were shot dead the other three surrendered, allowing Colin's masked helpers to disarm them and handcuff them around a tree.

Then the party host and guests were stripped of their jewels. Over fifteen million dollars' worth. Which was dumped into a large suitcase that was tossed into one of the getaway cars and driven off into oblivion.

What got André Colin caught, one month later, was a girl he'd fallen for. A pretty eighteen-year-old named Christine Boyer.

Colin met her, shortly before the Antibes jewel heist, in the Belgian port of Antwerp. She was working as a waitress at that time in a bar popular with Antwerp's night people. She was also, Colin learned when he showed interest, the mistress of a gambler who owned a piece of the bar.

One week after the big jewel robbery the gambler's body was found under a railway bridge. By the time it was found,

Colin had removed Christine Boyer from her bar job, taken her down to France, and installed her in a Paris apartment as his own mistress.

Three weeks later she tipped the police.

He almost escaped again, the same way as he had before: out of Christine Boyer's bedroom window into an alley. But it was a two-floor drop and Colin landed badly, breaking his ankle and losing his gun. He was searching for it, scrambling around in the darkness of the alley on his hands and knees, when the cops clubbed him unconscious.

That was everything we knew about André Colin. Other than his subsequent trial, incarceration in Fresnes, and escape. Not much. But there were a few obvious potential starting points in it. As leads went, they were frail. But with exploration they might improve in health. Fritz got on the phone to some of his far-flung contacts. After he had gotten the preliminary information we needed, I went next door to my own apartment and packed a bag.

When I returned with it, Fritz was back on the phone, digging for more information. That would be his primary job for the duration. It was the most vital one on any case, and one he could do without jeopardizing his still-weakened condition. Joelle and I left together and shared a cab out to Orly Airport. Arlette remained behind. She was taking on the job of handling Fritz's legwork in Paris for him, plus some supplemental telephoning from my apartment.

At Orly Joelle caught a plane south to Nice, where she had a trial to handle next morning. I took a plane flying north, to explore two of those potential leads.

7

It was bitter cold up there where France approached its border with Luxembourg. I was wearing a cashmere turtleneck under a heavy tweed jacket, with a corduroy cap on my head and a wool scarf around my neck. Even so I had to turn up the heating system of my rental car when I drove north from the airport outside Metz.

By the time I entered Longwy it was dark. That was when an outsider like myself could see how much the city had changed since André Colin had gone away to Italy and killed his father.

Back then the Longwy steel processing plants had worked full blast around the clock, their furnaces turning the night sky into a Dante's Inferno of flames and smoke. That prosperity had been obliterated over the intervening years by competition from lower-wage countries and labor-management disputes. All the steel plants were unlit empty shells now. Their contents had been dismantled and shipped to China.

The people of Longwy didn't have to look at those useless shells to know the difference. More than half of Longwy's work force was now unemployed.

From the window of Isabelle Colin's room, on the fifth floor of an old building near the railroad tracks, I could see high hills of iron ore and slag that hadn't been touched in so long, spindly trees had grown out of them.

"I'm afraid there's nothing I can tell you beyond what I've already told the police," she said. "They were here this afternoon."

"They're still here," I said, looking down at the two-door Renault in the narrow street below.

It had been there when I'd arrived. An unmarked car, but the two men in it wore CRS uniforms. They'd watched me park and enter the building. When I'd been halfway up the rickety stairway inside, one of them had come into the entry and looked up, watching until Madame Colin opened her door and let me in. He was back outside now. I watched him finish copying down my license number, walk to the unmarked car, and read it to his partner. Who would radio it in to their headquarters. It wouldn't take long to learn where I'd rented the car and what identification I'd used, and begin running a check on me.

"They're wasting their time and taxpayers' money," Isabelle Colin said. "My son would never come here."

I turned from the window and saw her returning across the room. "Here," she said, extending her open hand to me. There were three ten-franc coins in her palm.

Fritz had phoned her, soothing the way for me. There were few women, or men for that matter, that his rumbling voice and understanding tone couldn't soothe. That had accounted for his ability to extract confessions from suspects, back when he'd been a police detective. Fritz had relaxed Isabelle Colin to the point where she'd finally said that, since I would be showing up around her dinnertime, it would be kind of me to pick up a pizza for her from a place around the corner.

I shook my head. "You don't have to pay me for it, Madame Colin. Consider it a present."

There was genuine distress in her sudden frown. "But you must take this. I didn't ask you to get it because I can't afford it. I'm simply too lazy to climb down all those steps and up again when I don't have to. Just as I'm sometimes too lazy to make dinner for myself. Please.''

There are certain kinds of pride you don't buck. I took the three coins. Her smile was surprisingly youthful, breaking through a basic shyness. She carried the boxed pizza to the minimal kitchenette that took up one corner of her room.

It was a fairly large room, overcrowded with furniture and knickknacks from a time when her living quarters had been distributed through a number of rooms. All the furnishings were old, but none had been allowed to grow shabby.

A second corner served as her bedroom. A third was arranged as a center for her needlework. Five newly knitted sweaters were on a shelf there, three pullovers and two cardigans. On the round table in the center of the room was the beginning of another she'd been working on when I arrived.

"This pizza you bought is too big for me alone," she said from the kitchenette corner. "I usually get the medium size. Will you share it with me?"

"Yes," I said. "Thank you."

I watched her take her knitting from the round table and put it on the shelf with the finished sweaters. She was a sturdy, good-looking woman of not much more than fifty. She would have looked younger if it hadn't been for the deep lines around her eyes and mouth. They hadn't been put there by laughter. I asked if she sold her knitting locally.

"No, a woman who comes through the area every couple months buys them from me. She sells them to boutiques in Paris."

"Pay well?"

Again the shy smile. "Not too well, but it gives me a little added income. I still get my husband's insurance, but I've used up what I got from selling the apartment we used to live in."

"And from selling that property in Italy?"

"Yes." The smile was gone. Her eyes had a haunted look. "Please take a seat."

I sat down at the table while she covered it with an embroidered spread. She set the table for two, divided the sliced pizza evenly on our plates, added an opened bottle of wine. I filled our glasses as she sat down. It was good, inexpensive local red. The production of wine, and decorative ceramics, were two industries that still flourished in this area.

While we ate I asked, "Why are you so sure of what you said. That your son won't try to come here to see you?"

"Because he never has," she told me in a controlled tone. "Not here, and not when I was still living in the apartment."

"He ever phone you?"

"No. Never."

"When did you last have any contact with him?"

"Before they put him into that insane asylum in Italy," she told me in a voice that made me ease off on the questioning until after our meal.

She finished first, eating with a nervous quickness. Then she drank some wine and looked at me with those haunted eyes. "I tried to visit André when he was in that awful place," she said slowly. "In Reggio Emilia. But he refused to see me." Her voice was back under control. "I didn't see him again until I went to his trial last year. I *saw* him there, but he wouldn't talk to me."

"Perhaps he's ashamed with you," I suggested. "For the things he's done."

"Or perhaps he feels an anger against me. For causing him to be put in that place."

"You didn't put him there. He did that to himself."

"But it was my fault. I should have left my husband long before what happened. And taken André away with me. My husband was a violent man. He used to beat André, too. But it was his violence to me that André couldn't stand anymore."

Isabelle Colin took another drink from her glass. When she spoke again, there was an unexpected fierceness in her voice. "They should never have put my son into an insane asylum. He was only trying to protect me. I'm sure he was not crazy before that. They *made* him crazy, inside there."

I didn't argue that. "You think he blames you for it?"

"I don't know. How can I know? We've never spoken together since it happened."

I refilled our glasses. "People change, with time. He just might want to get in touch with you now. He's smart enough to know the cops will be watching this place. But he may phone—or have somebody else contact you for him. And he has certain information I need."

"Monsieur Donhoff told me you are working for André's lawyer."

"Arlette Alfani. Yes."

"I met her during his trial," Isabelle Colin said. "She took me to dinner. To talk about him. I didn't know anything that could help her much. But she tried to comfort me. A lovely young woman."

"Right now she's in trouble. The police suspect her of helping your son escape."

"That is ridiculous. Anyone who's met her could tell. She's not the sort who would do something like that."

"Your son could clear her," I said. "I want to talk to him about that."

"And to put him back in prison?"

"I'm not the police, Madame Colin."

She shook her head. "André won't get in touch with me. I'm almost certain of that."

I let that go for the moment, and asked about friends he'd had in this area, before the ill-fated trip to Italy. Anyone who'd been close enough for Colin to turn to for help now. But Isabelle Colin couldn't come up with a single name. He had never been one for making real friends, even as a boy.

"Did you ever meet Christine Boyer?" I asked. "The girl your son was living with when he was caught last year."

"No. She wasn't at his trial."

I knew that. Christine Boyer had vanished after squealing

on Colin to the police. They had looked for her and discovered she'd done a fast job of packing her things and getting out. If the gang involved with Colin in the Antibes jewel robbery hadn't found and killed her since, she had done a good job of hiding herself somewhere.

Now that Colin was out she had more reason than ever to continue to hide. Colin had a record of retaliating against people who'd done him dirt. That was one reason I was going to try tracing her. Because Colin might be hunting her, too.

The other reason was that she might be able to supply information about circumstances surrounding that gem haul—and about other people in it who'd had reason to bust Colin out of prison.

Before leaving Isabelle Colin I gave her my card. I wrote Fritz's phone number on it above my own. "This one belongs to my partner," I told her. "Monsieur Donhoff is pretty sure to be in, and I might not be. Please call him if you hear from your son. Or learn anything more about him."

She didn't respond to that, and didn't touch the card when I put it on the table between us.

"If the police try to take him," I said as I stood up, "he'll put up a fight and they'll have to kill him. I only want to ask him some questions. And maybe I can talk him into surrendering while I'm at it. If he's willing, I can arrange for him to be taken into custody—alive. Think about it."

She did think about it, as she walked me to her door. "It is a horrible thing for a mother to say," she told me when we reached it, "but finally . . . after everything that has been done to him and what he's become . . . my son may be better off dead."

And then, without warning, Isabelle Colin began to cry.

I took her in my arms and she pressed her face against my chest, holding on to me while the sobs racked her whole body.

I didn't let go of her until the weeping ceased and she had control of herself again. She was apologizing as I led her to a chair and sat her down. I got her wineglass and watched her take a healthy sip from it. We looked at each other, but neither of us found anything more to say. She was still sitting there, taking small sips of her wine, when I let myself out.

The surveillance car was still there when I came out of the building, but neither of the two uniformed cops was inside it. They were on either side of the building's doorway, waiting for me.

One held a compact submachine gun on me at waist level. The other saluted and asked politely for my identification papers.

"You must have gotten my identity over your radio by now," I said as I gave him my open wallet.

He nodded. "We have to make sure you're the one who rented that car over there. It could have been stolen since then." He looked at my picture and my face, comparing, and then flipped to my investigator's license and nodded again. "They told us you're a private detective. What were you seeing Madame Colin about?"

"I'm working for her son's attorney."

"Doing what?"

You don't tell a French cop that he has no right to ask any question he wants to ask. I said, "Trying to find out where Colin is. Like you. And making as little progress."

"Think his mother knows?"

"No. And he isn't likely to come see her. You're waiting around here for nothing."

"I wish we didn't already know that." He gave me back my wallet. "Where are you going to try next?"

"I haven't figured that one out yet," I said.

I got back to the airport outside Metz with less than ten minutes left before the last plane of the night that I could take to get to Brussels. When I landed, there was only one car rental firm still open at Brussels Airport. All they had available was a large, expensive Mercedes. I took it and headed for the E-10 expressway.

It was snowing in Belgium. Big wet flakes that fell lazily out of a cold mist and melted when they hit the roadway. Nothing serious enough to slow my driving much. But it was hard to believe I had been swimming in the sea under a hot sun that morning before turning on the noon TV news.

A glance at the dashboard clock told me it was about to become the next morning. It was shortly after midnight when I got to Antwerp.

8

THE BANGKOK BAR WAS OFF FALCON PLEIN NEAR THE COM-
plex of docks straddling the River Scheldt and stretching north
to the Dutch border.

It was on Old Man's Street. The block was crowded with
other bars: Irish Kitty's, the San Francisco Saloon, Old Sail-
or's Café, the Tangier Ferry, the Istanbul, Copenhagen Taxi,
Charlie Brown's, the Hong Kong Club. Antwerp is as international as they come. A terminal for the network of barge
canals that connect the Atlantic Ocean with the Mediterranean and the Black Sea, as well as one of Europe's busiest
seaports and the world center for diamond cutting.

The interior of the Bangkok was warm and dry, a noisy,
smoky oasis after the cold, wet night outside. I unbuttoned
my jacket and stuffed my scarf and cap into its side pockets
while I looked around. There was nothing remotely Asian
about the place to justify its name. Just solid, old-fashioned
Flemish comfort. Dim yellowish lighting from lace-shaded
lamps. Big wooden tables covered with carpet material
scorched by cigars and cigarettes and matches that had missed
the brass ashtrays over the years. Cushioned armchairs. A
long zinc-topped bar. A bead curtain across the deep end of
the main room, through which you could see a gang of men
around a pool table.

The place drew an interesting mixture. There was a group

of barge families around two tables pulled together—men, women, teenagers, a four-year-old curled up asleep in a chair. Other tables were taken by fashionably dressed couples from town, a bunch of reasonably well-behaved young guys in motorcycle gear, and some men who might have been waiters who'd just gotten off work, or thieves having a drink before going to work.

The crowd along the bar was mostly dockworkers and crewmen from seagoing vessels. There were two hookers on barstools, one in her teens and the other in her forties. They seemed equally popular with the crowd. Two waitresses and two barmaids, dressed alike in miniskirts, knee boots, and frilly, low-cut blouses, were being kept busy taking care of everybody. Whatever else went on behind the scene at the Bangkok Bar, it wasn't in the doldrums up front.

The woman I was looking for wasn't there. Might as well do some work while I waited for her. I found a space against the bar and wedged myself into it. The barmaid who came to serve me was a big, buxom redhead. She wasn't wearing a bra. Neither were the waitresses. It gave the customers something to do, watching them prance back and forth.

I ordered a genever and beer, speaking English. Though Belgium is officially a bilingual country—French and Flemish—around Antwerp people don't like anyone who speaks French and they'll often pretend not to understand it. If you can't handle Flemish, the preferred alternative is English, the second language of almost everyone in the city.

The red-haired barmaid even caught my accent: "American or Canadian?"

"American."

"I like Americans," she said, smiling at me. She went to fill my order.

When she came back with my drinks, I added a large tip to the price. She gave me another smile. "Americans are so generous. What is your name?"

"Pete."

"Well, Pete, my name is Alma."

"Isn't Christine Boyer working tonight?" I asked her.

She looked blank. "Who?"

I repeated the name. "She's a waitress here. Or was, last time I was in."

"I never heard of her. How long ago was this?"

"More than a year ago."

"Ah! I have only worked here two months. But Marie must have known her." Alma pointed to the other barmaid, near the far end of the bar. "She has been here longer than any of us. More than three years." When I picked up my glasses, Alma added quickly, "But come back. I will take good care of you."

I found a place at the end of the bar, drank the genever and chased it with sips of beer while I watched Marie work. She was about thirty, slender, and blond, with a pert nose and large beautiful mouth. Her face reminded me of Brigitte Bardot.

She finally took a short cigarette break at my end of the bar. When she got her lighter out, I took it from her hand and snapped it on, holding it near her cigarette. She studied me briefly, then nodded her thanks and leaned forward and let me light her cigarette for her.

"Hello, Marie," I said. "I'm trying to locate Christine Boyer."

She snatched the cigarette from her lips, coughing on the smoke she'd inhaled. I reached across the bar and patted her on the back. When the spasm ended, she studied me with narrowed eyes. "I don't know where Christine is. She went away somewhere and never came back."

Her English had a definite French accent.

I smiled at her and switched to French. "You sound to me like a Parisienne."

She was startled again. "You're French, too?"

"Of course. My name's Pierre-Ange. And you're Marie—what?"

"Vernon. Marie Vernon."

"Pleased to meet you. Was I right? You're from Paris?"

"I lived there, before I came here." Our speaking French together had brought her guard down a bit. "But originally I'm from Toulouse. What are you—a journalist or from the French police?"

"Neither. I'm just a private detective, doing a job for an attorney. It's nothing complicated or dangerous. My client simply wants to talk to Christine Boyer. That's all."

"I *don't* know where she is. That's the truth."

"But I understand you did know her quite well, in the past."

Marie Vernon's eyes narrowed again. "Who told you that?"

"Look," I said, "I understand you can't talk here." I got out one of my business cards—the French version—and a pen. I turned the card over and wrote the name of the Antwerp hotel where Arlette had reserved a room for me. "I'm staying at this hotel. Call me there and we'll get together, very private. I'll pay you *very* well, for just a few minutes of talk. Anything you know about Christine Boyer or her past."

"I never knew her that well. Just to work with here." Marie Vernon was growing increasingly tense. "I did put her up when she first came to Antwerp. But for less than a week. Only until her man got her an apartment of her own."

"You can tell me where she came here *from*, for starters."

She glanced away nervously, toward the rear of the place, then back to me, not speaking.

"And," I added, "you could tell me who some of her friends were."

"I didn't know any of them."

"Yes, you did," I said. "You knew her man. Alfred Streuvels." That was the name of the gambler who'd been found dead after André Colin took a fancy to Christine Boyer.

Marie Vernon started to say something, but stopped herself. "Excuse me . . ." She came around the end of the bar and hurried past me toward the rear of the main room. I watched her go through the bead curtains there and around the group of men at the pool table. She opened a door in the back of that room, went in, and shut it behind her.

I finished my genever, took another sip of beer, leaned my back against the bar, and waited.

After a few minutes that rear door opened and Marie Vernon emerged into the poolroom. She came back through the bead curtains to my end of the bar, holding herself stiffly. Customers nearby called to her for service, but she ignored them. She stood there looking at me. Her eyes were defiant and a little frightened. Her mouth was no longer beautiful. The lips were almost invisible, sucked in against her teeth.

"I take it," I said mildly, "you didn't get permission to tell me about Christine Boyer."

Marie Vernon looked past me toward the back of the place.

I looked in the same direction and finally saw something about the Bangkok Bar that went with its name.

9

TWO MEN HAD COME OUT OF THE DOOR AT THE REAR OF THE poolroom. They were followed by a third man. He in turn was followed by two more, these sticking close to his back. The first two and the couple bringing in the rear were obvious bodyguards. Medium tall, young, athletic builds, alert expressions.

They were Asians and so was the man they were protecting.

I couldn't be sure what kind of Asians. That's as difficult as deciding what country a European comes from. Someone who looks Greek can turn out to be a Swede and a face you peg as Chinese can be Malaysian.

But I decided, tentatively, that the four bodyguards could be from Thailand. Influenced partly by the name of the bar but also by the way they moved. Like Thai boxers. Ready to strike out with their feet. As well as their elbows and knees and any blunt, sharp, or explosive weapons they might have concealed on them.

The man they were protecting was short, compact, with a smooth, plump, thoughtful face. He could have been anywhere in his forties. He wore rimless glasses and an exquisitely tailored black business suit with a discreet, barely visible gray stripe. He didn't move like his bodyguards. His stiff, brisk walk was that of a man who spends most of his time sitting behind a desk. He stopped when he reached me. Two of his bodyguards flanked him looking in my direction. The other pair turned around behind him to watch the rest of the room.

Their boss gave me a polite smile, verging on friendly. "You are inquiring about Christine Boyer," he said in flawless French. "But you've come to the wrong place to look for her. No one here can help you."

"Not even you?" I said.

"I'm afraid not, unfortunately." He seemed unruffled by the subject. "The police were here earlier, inquiring about the same thing. I had to tell them what I am telling you. Christine worked here briefly, a long time ago. None of us knew her well, and we haven't heard anything of her since she went away."

"With André Colin."

"So I've been given to understand, after she left. I imagine he is the reason you are interested in Christine. The same reason for the authorities' interest in her. But I didn't know him, nor of Christine's connection with him."

"You could know other things about her past that might help me."

He shook his head. "If I had any useful information— which I do not—I would give it to the police, rather than a private detective. A man who owns a bar in any city needs to preserve good relations with the authorities."

"But you didn't tell them anything either."

"Because I know nothing worth telling." He glanced pointedly at his all-gold wristwatch. It looked like a Piaget. "Now, if you'll forgive me, I have pressing business elsewhere. I hope you will not bother my help with further questions. Please. They know even less than I. And they are supposed to be tending to my clientele, not engaging in pointless conversations."

With that he abruptly turned away and started for the

Bangkok Bar's entrance. As before, two of his protectors led the way and the other pair swung in behind him.

A moment after they went out into the night the woman I'd been waiting for came in.

She was a lean woman of forty-seven, wearing a rain hat, trench coat, and thick-soled, flat-heeled boots. Her name was Pauline Jacobs. She had a pleasant, small-featured face with nothing remarkable about it. Being easy to overlook and hard to remember was one of the qualities that helped Pauline earn a living for herself and her two kids.

She adjusted the strap of her big shoulder bag as she looked around the place. Her gaze passed over me and searched the rest of the room. Then she shrugged to herself and made a face, as though she didn't see whoever she was looking for. She went to the other end of the bar and ordered a drink.

At my end of the bar Marie Vernon was saying, "You heard him—now please go away and stop bothering me." My card was still on the bar between us. She pushed it across to me.

I pushed it back to her. "You may change your mind later."

Marie Vernon picked up my card, tore it in half, and dropped the pieces on the floor behind the bar. Then she went to wait on thirsty customers.

At the other end of the bar Pauline Jacobs had finished her drink. She left without looking back. My beer glass was still half-full. I carried it down the bar and signaled Alma, the red-haired barmaid.

She came over happily. "You're back!"

I nodded and smiled and ordered another genever. Alma brought it promptly. "I saw you talking to the boss," she said. "You should have told me you know him."

"I don't know him very well," I said. "I can't even remember his name."

Alma laughed. "Neither can I. Not all of it. Too complicated. Everybody just calls him Huang."

"That his family name?"

"I'm not sure."

I took a sip of genever and a swallow of beer. "Isn't it on your paycheck?"

"No, Huang has an accountant who signs those."

"Huang—sounds Chinese."

Alma shrugged that she didn't know. A customer yelled for her. She went to take care of him. I knocked back the rest of my genever, put on my cap and scarf, and went out.

The snow had changed to a thin drizzle outside. Just as cold. I looked up and down Old Man's Street. A couple of the bars had shut down. I didn't see Pauline Jacobs and I didn't waste my time looking for her. I walked away from the Bangkok Bar. When she saw I wasn't followed, she emerged from the dark, recessed doorway of a closed tattoo parlor diagonally across the street.

She trailed after me slowly, not trying to catch up until I was around the corner unlocking my rented Mercedes. When she reached me, I said, "I'm starving."

"I know a good café that's open all night."

"Get in and show me the way. I'll bring you back to your car after."

When we were both inside the Mercedes, Pauline reached into her shoulder bag and handed me a bulky manila envelope. I removed what was in it. A small Sig/Sauer .380 caliber automatic in a belt holster. I checked to make sure the magazine held all seven loads and the safety was on.

"Dump it in a sewer when you're through here," Pauline said. "It can't be traced to me or anyone I know." She watched me belt it on my hip, under the jacket. "But if the police find you carrying it, you're in big trouble, you know. Sure you want to take that chance?"

"No—but I am sure I don't want to get caught in a corner

without it. Not by the kind of people Dédé Colin associates with."

The all-night café was on Schippers Street. We were still close to the harbor. The smell of the river carried a hint of the North Sea in it. From inside the café you could look through its big window and see the dock cranes and straddle carriers looming above nearby rooftops.

There were several customers at the counter and two couples at the front table. The other tables were empty. We went to the last one in the back. Pauline took off her coat and hat and hung them on a wall peg. She was dressed in an inconspicuous tweed jacket and skirt. Other than a plain wristwatch she wore no jewelry. She never did when she was working.

I hung up my cap and scarf, sat down with Pauline, and looked at the menu. Pauline said the beef stew was excellent. When the waiter came, I ordered that. Pauline said all she wanted was some tea. The waiter went away. I asked if she'd noticed the five men who had left the Bangkok Bar when she was about to enter it.

She had, of course. "I didn't get much of a look at their faces, though. The light outside wasn't good enough."

"Four of them are bodyguards," I said. "It's the fifth one I'm interested in. Seems he owns the place. Name's Huang. I don't know if that's his family name."

"It is," Pauline told me. "The full name is Huang Yok Lin." She got a notebook from her shoulder bag and printed the name, tore out the page, and gave it to me.

I looked at it and put it in my pocket. "Chinese?"

"Yes. But from Thailand."

"You didn't know any of this when Fritz called you earlier. You've been busy earning your fee."

"What fee? From what Fritz told me your client is family. I don't charge other detectives when I do work for their families, and neither do you. Except for expenses." Pauline smiled. "Like between dentists, except sometimes it's harder than pulling a tooth."

"Arlette is not exactly family," I said.

"You spending much time with other women?"

"Not lately," I admitted.

"Then she's family. It doesn't take a marriage license, Pete."

Pauline's kids were from an alcoholic husband she'd walked out on but never divorced. She'd wound up living with a Brussels private detective she had gone to work for as a secretary. After he'd been killed in an auto accident Pauline had taken over his business. We had called on each other's services before. For my money she had become one of the best private investigators in Belgium.

She took a photograph out of her shoulder bag. It was a profile shot of the man I'd talked to in the Bangkok Bar. "This is a blowup from a newspaper photo. Taken at a charity affair. He's established a reputation as a civic-minded businessman in the eight years he's lived in Antwerp. Always willing to help a good cause."

"Is he the sole owner of the bar?"

Pauline nodded. "Since his partner died without heirs."

"Alfred Streuvels—the gambler Christine Boyer lived with."

"Right. It seems that Huang only took Streuvels in as his partner because he needed a Belgian front man to open a business when he first came here. Huang doesn't need that anymore. He's become a Belgian citizen."

"Any other businesses, beside the bar?"

"He's gotten heavily into real estate. And he has an import-export business. It's called the HYL-Orient Trading Company."

"H.Y.L.—his initials."

Pauline nodded. "Those are his legitimate businesses. I talked to one of my contacts in the police. He says they suspect Huang may also be involved with some organization bringing illegal immigrants into Europe from the East. Suspicion is all they have. No proof, and Huang's acquired too many prominent friends to be hustled without strong evidence.''

"Is he involved in stolen gems, too?" I asked.

"I don't know. That's all the digging I did on him. Fritz told me to see what I could find out about Christine Boyer and the place where she used to work. I didn't know you'd be this interested in Huang.''

"I am now," I told her.

"So I'll dig deeper, tomorrow.''

"What have you gotten on Christine Boyer?"

"Damn little. She worked eight months at the Bangkok Bar. She hasn't been back here since she went away with Colin, that I've been able to discover. Nobody seems to have heard from or about her since then. And so far I haven't turned up anyone who was close enough to her before that to have information about her background.''

"I think I have," I said. "There's a woman who works at the bar. Marie Vernon. See what you can get me on her.''

The waiter came back with our orders. While I ate, we discussed Pauline's next priorities. I gave my meal most of my attention. It deserved it. The beef stew was as delicious as Pauline had promised. I finished it off feeling the resurgence of energy I wanted. A strong cup of black coffee with my dessert did the rest of the job, prodding my nerves back on full alert.

When we left the café, I took Pauline to her car. She drove home to get some sleep.

But my night wasn't finished yet.

⊠ **10** ⊠

OUT ON THE DARK RIVER, POOLS OF LIGHT MET, MERGED, and separated as a canal barge and a deep-sea freighter passed each other. The barge eased in toward a mooring spot near the Royers Sluis and the ship continued on its way along the Scheldt toward the open sea. That was the only traffic out on the water. There was none at all between the shuttered, unlit buildings of the harbor's landside complex except my rented Mercedes and the taxicab I was tailing.

The cab's rear lights made it easy for me to follow it from a good distance behind. I had the Mercedes's lights off, making it hard to spot among the deep shadows if the cabdriver happened to check his rearview mirror. There was no reason he should unless Marie Vernon had asked him to, and she hadn't acted wary when she'd come out of the Bangkok Bar and climbed into the cab.

It had picked her up there at 2:30 A.M. as the bar was closing. She'd come out wearing a sheer plastic raincoat over a pants suit and carrying an umbrella against the cold rain. The direction the cab had taken from there had come as a surprise. Over to the city end of the port and into its maze of wharves, dockyards, and warehouses, zigzagging among its canal terminals and locks.

The harbor area was dead quiet and the cab was not. I was able to follow by its sound as well as its taillights. The Mercedes justified its high rental in there. The purr of its motor wouldn't be heard twenty feet away.

The cab cruised past the Bonaparte and Willem wharves, curved around the Kattendijk Dock and the end of the Royers Sluis. I threaded after it between a dry dock and a long quay where a mammoth suction dredger and two sand barges were moored. The cab pulled to a stop at a wharf with a two-floor warehouse on it. I parked in the cavernous murk between a discharge crane and a moored pile-driving derrick, cut my motor, and watched.

A cargo ship in need of rust removal and repainting was tied up along one side of the wharf's warehouse. I could just make out its name and home port painted on the stern. The *Jade Rose*, out of Singapore. At the far end of the wharf a sleek canal barge in mint condition was moored. There was a company sign on the land end of the warehouse: HYL-ORIENT TRADING COMPANY.

Marie Vernon climbed out of the cab and opened her umbrella as the driver executed a backing turn. The cab came past me and headed back out of the harbor area. I left the Mercedes and moved quickly and quietly toward the wharf. Marie Vernon looked at the closed entrance of the dark warehouse and called out something I couldn't hear distinctly.

There was no answer to her call. She looked at the cargo ship and then toward an open passage along the other side of the warehouse. Then she shrugged and went around the front of the warehouse, taking the open passage toward the far end of the wharf. I followed, closing the gap between us some more, sticking to cover in case she stopped and turned around.

She did, halfway along the passage. But she didn't spot me. I was frozen in shadow against the warehouse wall. She called again and this time I was close enough to make it out.

"Lee?"

Still no response. She didn't act worried about it, just surprised. When she turned and continued along the passage, I trailed after her again.

The canal barge at the end of the wharf had the customary long, wide deckhouse on its afterdeck. The condition of the barge's mooring cables indicated it hadn't moved from the wharf in a long time. But the exterior of the deckhouse had a refurbished polish. There were no lights on inside it. Marie Vernon walked up the gangplank, took a key from her handbag, and unlocked the door at the stern of the deckhouse.

Then she glanced back down at the wharf and called out one more time: "Lee?"

Another shrug when that went unanswered. I watched her close her umbrella. The second she stepped inside the deckhouse I went up the gangplank. I was crossing the deck when she switched on the interior light of the room she'd entered. The windows of the rest of the deckhouse remained dark.

She shut the door behind her, but I didn't hear it being relocked from inside. I drew the little Sig/Sauer automatic from its holster, thumbed off the safety, and tried the door handle with my left hand. It wasn't locked. I opened the door and went in, making as much noise as butter melting.

The room inside was a spacious salon. It was furnished in basic Scandinavian modern with expensive touches of Asia here and there. The dark-colored lotus-patterned carpet covering much of the teak floor looked like an eighteenth-century Khotan, and was probably genuine since Huang could obviously afford it. The doorway between the salon and the dark forward parts of the deckhouse had been rebuilt in the shape of a Chinese moon gate. On the other side of the room a rosewood altar supported an ebony and ivory statue of the dark Hindu goddess Kali, ambivalent giver of both bountiful life and hideous death.

Marie Vernon was alone near a lacquered table inlaid with a coiled dragon in mother-of-pearl. She stood with her back to me, taking off her raincoat.

I lowered the gun beside my thigh, shut the door behind

me, and said, "Lee doesn't seem to be around tonight, whoever Lee is."

She dropped the raincoat on the carpet and spun to face me, eyes and mouth wide with shock. But she was quick to recover. "Lee is the night watchman here," she told me with a sharp rasp to her tone. "He's got a gun and he's an expert with it. If you're not gone before he gets back, he'll probably kill you."

"I've got a gun, too," I said and showed it to her, raising it just a bit. "It may be smaller than Lee's, but it doesn't give kisses, so don't even think about yelling for him."

I went around the salon and closed the four window curtains so no one could see us from outside. Marie Vernon stayed put and watched me do it. I took a stand by the table, where I could watch her and the door to the deck at the same time. I kicked her dropped raincoat away from between us. It left a large wet spot on the pricey Khotan. I said, "Sit down and tell me about Christine Boyer."

She just looked at me, frozen-faced.

I put my hand against her chest and pushed her off balance. She fell backward, flailing her arms, expecting to hit the floor. But there was a big easy chair behind her. She landed in that, looking surprised.

"Talk to me," I snapped. "Now. I don't have until dawn."

"I told you before—I don't know where she is."

"Maybe not, but you do know the rest. Where she's from, for a start."

"No." Marie Vernon shook her head to emphasize it, but I didn't sense enough conviction. She shrank back again when I moved in on her and pointed the automatic at her face. "Please don't," she bleated. "I'm afraid of guns."

"More afraid of something else, or you'd be answering my questions by now."

"I *told* you!"

"You told me lies. Was Christine Boyer from France or Italy?"

Her eyes narrowed a little. I could see her brain at work thinking up more lies. "She has to be from one or the other," I said. "She did live awhile with Colin, and they must have talked to each other now and then. Colin knows French because that's what he is. And some Italian because he spent time in an Italian nuthouse. He doesn't speak any other language."

But Marie Vernon was no longer listening to me or looking at my automatic. She was looking at something directly behind me, and her face had gone deathly pale.

I wasn't stupid enough to try spinning around. For which I gave thanks when the cold metal of a large gun muzzle pressed lightly against the back of my neck.

A voice behind me said, "Christine doesn't know any Italian. We always spoke French together."

🔲 11 🔲

"LAY THE GUN DOWN ON THE TABLE." HIS TONE WAS CRISP and cool. "After you put the safety on."

I did what he'd told me to, placing the automatic on the dragon's mother-of-pearl head and taking my hand away from it.

"Now go over against the wall next to Marie."

I did that, too, and then turned around and looked at him. Dédé Colin looked back at me with that amused smile and unblinking stare.

He was no taller than my shoulder, but he was built solid and looked agile. He was wearing a merchant seaman's outfit. Dark blue watch cap, sweater, and pea coat. Black dungarees and boots. The coat was open. His left hand rested lightly on the checkered butt of a large revolver stuck under his belt.

His right hand held a short-barreled repeating shotgun at waist level. He had it tilted up at my face so I could look into it. It was like staring into the end of a dark tunnel with my death waiting deep inside it.

My mouth was dry and my palms felt damp. I wondered why it's never the other way around when fear knocks your mechanisms out of kilter. I made myself look away, at the moon gate doorway behind him that connected to the dark parts of the deckhouse.

Colin nodded. "I was waiting in there when she came aboard. Spotted you behind her." He transferred his smile to Marie Vernon. "I checked with your roommate. She told me you're spending nights with Huang again. He use up his other mistresses and decide to take you back?"

Her voice squeaked with terror: "*You're* why Lee isn't around."

Colin laughed. "He's around, Marie. Under the wharf with the rest of the garbage."

The shotgun had remained aimed at me when he looked at her. His eyes flicked back to me. "Who are you and why are you interested in Christine?"

I told him my name. "I'm a private detective and I'm working for your ex-attorney. Arlette Alfani."

"How do I know that's so?"

"I was with her when your friend from Fresnes, Roux, came around to give her your message. Roux told her if she didn't come see you Monday you'd get yourself another lawyer to deal with the government."

Colin nodded. He didn't need time to think over whether that constituted proof I was what I said I was. His head might or might not be off center, but it wasn't slow. "That still doesn't tell me why you're interested in Christine."

"Your little trick put Arlette Alfani in trouble," I told him. "A written or verbal statement from you that she didn't have any part in your escape—and who *did*—will get her out of that trouble. I was looking for Christine Boyer because she might have a lead to you. Now I don't need to find her. You're here. Can we talk about it?"

"That's interesting," he said thoughtfully. "You're trying to find Christine—and so am I." He looked to Marie Vernon again. "If she's contacted anybody around here since I got taken, it would be *you*."

Marie Vernon was gripping the arms of the chair so hard, her knuckles stuck out like bleached stones. "She *never* got in touch after she went away with you. I *swear* that's true, on my mother's life.''

''On *your* life, Marie,'' Colin said softly. ''Tell me something that's not true—just once—and you're dead.'' He side-stepped away from me. When he was on the other side of her, he pointed the shotgun at her head. She shut her eyes and raised a forearm across her face. Colin told her quietly, ''Drop your arm and look at me.''

She obeyed him instantly.

''You see,'' Colin told me, ''you didn't scare her enough. I do.''

The shotgun wasn't close enough for me to grab for it without taking a long step first. His reputation didn't encourage me to make the try.

Marie Vernon was taking deep breaths through her open mouth. Not enough of the air seemed to be getting as far as her lungs. ''I don't know where Christine went, Dédé,'' she said in a voice as fragile as the last ice of spring. ''Nobody does. Huang had a lot of people looking, for a long time.''

''You're sure they didn't find her.''

''Not a trace.''

''Then she's still alive somewhere.'' Colin seemed relieved—perhaps even happy about that. Which was peculiar, if his reason for seeking Christine Boyer was to kill her for squealing on him. I filed that away for thinking about later.

Marie Vernon said, ''She's alive as far as I know.''

''As far as *Huang* knows?'' Colin demanded softly.

She couldn't get her voice working again. Finally she just nodded.

''All right,'' Colin said, ''that tells me part of what I came to find out.'' He gave me his full attention again. ''I've got to find Christine. It's hard for me to move around searching. I've got to spend too much time keeping out of sight. So I need help. You're looking for her anyway.''

''Not anymore. It's you I was looking for.''

"You're a private detective. Clients pay you to find out things for them. Okay, I can pay you whatever it takes."

I shook my head. "I don't work for blood money. And I'm already working for Mademoiselle Alfani. I'll trade you. Help me clear her name and then I'll see what I can do about finding Christine Boyer." I was playing for time at that point. Waiting for Colin to do something careless so I could jump him. But he hadn't shown any tendency toward carelessness so far.

"Sounds like a good deal," Colin said, "but let's turn it around. You find Christine for me and then I'll clear Alfani for you."

"What do you want her for?" I asked him.

"That's between Christine and me. I just want you to look for her. That job doesn't include prying into my private business."

We studied each other. He wasn't going to bend. I decided it didn't matter. Whichever way we made the arrangement I had no intention of delivering my part of it. If Colin wanted Christine Boyer that badly, and thought I was searching for her, he'd have to keep in contact with me. Next time we met I'd be better prepared. Ready to take him off balance. The way he'd taken me, this time.

Once I had him under control, I could lie some more. Offer to not turn him over to the law, in exchange for his clearing Arlette. I didn't mind lying to Dédé Colin.

"It's a deal," I told him.

⊠ **12** ⊠

COLIN LOOKED NEITHER PLEASED NOR DISPLEASED. HIS EYES tried to open my skull and have a look at what was inside. I didn't think he could. I used to play pretty good poker. Finally he nodded and said, "You'll find Christine for me."

"I'll give it a try. It's regarded as unethical in my business to promise a client results you're not sure you can deliver."

Taking on this particular client, under these weird circumstances, put my professional ethics on a par with grave robbing. Okay. I've done worse on occasion. Necessity is the mother of artful dodging.

"How do I contact you when I learn something?" I asked him.

He grinned at me. "I'll do the contacting. Just tell me where."

I told him the name of my Antwerp Hotel. "If I've left there, call one of my numbers in France. I have to reach into my pocket for those. Don't get nervous about it."

"I never get nervous," Colin said.

I took out one of my cards and gave it to him. It had my Paris and Riviera numbers. "Try the Paris number first. When I'm not there, the answering machine is on. Leave a message where I can call you or when you'll call back."

Colin slid my card in his pocket without any relaxation of wariness.

"The problem is," I said, "I don't know where to look for her. Right now I'm at a dead end. I need more information."

"I'm at a dead end, too," Colin said. "All I've found out here is Christine's still alive. Huang didn't find her."

"Why would she be dead if he found her?"

"He might've killed her, trying to get information out of her."

"What information?"

"You don't need to know that."

"It might help me find her."

"You have to manage without it," Colin said flatly.

I had a hunch what the information would be about. Knowing the details on that, it occurred to me, could prove interesting. For a couple of reasons. But Colin wasn't about to budge on that subject.

It was at that point that I began changing my mind about just pretending to hunt for Christine Boyer. I wanted to talk to her.

"Where were you planning to look for her next?" I asked Colin.

"I was hoping Marie would know something I could figure out my next move from. But you heard—she doesn't."

"If she told you the truth."

"Sure she did," Colin said with absolute certainty. "Marie knows if she lies to me, I'll come back after I find out and kill her. Don't you know that, Marie?"

She nodded again. Jerking her head up and down as though any movement took a great effort of will. She had been sitting there like a block of wood while we talked over her and about her. Her face was drained blank. But her eyes weren't. They watched Colin's face every second. Terrified eyes. I decided she hadn't lied to him—and wouldn't.

"I need something to work with," I told Colin. "Her background at least. Any friends she might still be in touch with."

Colin shook his head. "Christine's pretty much a loner, like me. Marie here's the only one got close to her at all. Except that gambler, Streuvels—and Christine didn't like him that much."

Pauline Jacobs was right—it was sometimes harder than pulling teeth. "You spoke French together. Is that where she came here from?"

"Paris. That's why I took her back there. She likes it in Paris better than here."

"Is Paris where she's from originally? Or some other part of France?"

"Christine's not French, originally," Colin said. "She talks French with a funny little accent. But I don't know where from."

I stared at him. "You were her lover and you never asked her?"

"No, why should I? I don't like people asking me questions. So I don't ask any when it's something I don't need to know about. Christine's a girl and I liked her, that's all. Why would I have to know where she was from?"

"It might help me to know," I said, and nodded at Marie Vernon. "I think she knows."

He looked at her. "Do you?" When she only went on staring at him, like a mouse looking at a large snake, he said, "Tell us, Marie."

She opened her mouth a couple times, but nothing came out.

"*Marie* . . ." Colin growled.

"Vietnam," she blurted weakly. "Christine was born in Vietnam."

Colin was startled. It was the closest to a show of emotion I'd seen in him yet. "What are you talking about?" he demanded. "Christine isn't any kind of Oriental. She's European. Light brown hair, blue eyes . . ."

"But her mother was Vietnamese," Marie Vernon said. "The way Christine looks comes from her. father."

"You're making this up." Colin said it softly, but something in his face made her shrink back in her chair again.

"No—I *swear* it's so. Christine told me once. Her father was a soldier in Vietnam and his name was Boyer. That's all she knows about him. Not even if he was French or American or some other kind of Caucasian. Her mother never wanted to talk about him."

A few odd threads were beginning to weave together in a potentially interesting pattern. Huang and his security men were Asian. The two guys who had rented the chopper that had flown Colin away from prison had been Asian. And now it turned out Christine Boyer was from Asia.

I asked Colin, "Who supplied those masked gunmen you used for the Antibes jewel heist?"

"Your job's finding Christine," he said coldly. "Not asking me things the cops want to know."

"My guess is it's the same gang that arranged your escape from Fresnes. Huang?"

"If you need any more from Marie get on with it. We're not going to have much more time here before we get the kind of company you won't like and I won't either."

"I need *a lot* more," I told Colin. "Like do you happen to have a picture of Christine?"

He didn't. I looked at Marie Vernon. She shook her head. "How'd she get from Vietnam to Paris?" I asked her.

She tore her eyes away from Colin for a second. "I don't know—Christine never talked to me about that." Her eyes switched back to Colin quickly. "She *didn't*."

"Did you know her before she came here? In Paris?"

Her eyes stayed on Colin this time as she answered me. "No."

"What brought her from there to the Bangkok Bar?"

"Huang knew Christine in Paris. He's the one imported her to Antwerp. Because his partner, Streuvels, fell for her after Huang introduced him to her. One time when they were down in Paris together.''

"According to Colin here,'' I said, "Christine didn't much like either Antwerp or Streuvels. So why did she stay here so long?''

"Huang had some kind of hold on her,'' Marie Vernon said, and answered my next question before I could ask it: "I've got no idea what it was.''

I looked to Colin. "Do you know?''

He said he didn't. I said, "She was your mistress for a while, for God's sake. What *did* you talk about?''

Colin shrugged a shoulder. His left one. The shotgun in his right hand didn't budge. "We never talked much. I gave her presents and enough dough to do any shopping she wanted. And she gave me what I wanted. We weren't into deep conversations.''

"Sparkling relationship.''

"Good enough. We didn't have any problems.''

"Then why did she squeal on you?'' I slipped that in on the chance the answer might spill out of him before he could stop it. More likely he would just tell me that was something else I didn't need to know. But Colin didn't do either. I watched him give the question some thought. Then he shook his head and said, "I don't know.''

It was odd. I got the feeling that not only didn't he know, but that he hadn't given it much thought before. I looked back to Marie Vernon. "Huang go down to Paris often?''

"Now and then. Every few months.''

"On business?''

"I guess so. He doesn't tell me about that, and I don't ask.''

That could be true and so could what Colin had said about himself and Christine Boyer. Relationships between criminals and their girlfriends don't usually involve the kind of intimacy that includes sharing secrets. Whatever most underworld women know about their men's professional activities tends to be learned indirectly.

"Huang didn't pick up his fluent French on occasional visits," I said. "Did he ever live in France?"

"I think so," Marie Vernon said. "But I'm not sure."

There was much more I wanted to know, but my probe for information ended right there.

"Lee?" a voice that sounded like Huang's called from the wharf. And a second later: "Marie?"

"*Merde,*" Colin whispered.

He didn't seem overly upset. Just annoyed by something he'd been expecting and now had to deal with. About the same degree of annoyance I'd felt when some cracked roof tiles had finally begun leaking rainwater into my attic. No more, no less.

He swept my automatic off the table. It landed on the carpet leaning against a fold of Marie Vernon's damp raincoat. "I'll be in touch," he told me, and reached the closed door to the deck with three long strides. He hit the light switch beside it, plunging the salon into blackness. Then he opened the door and went out fast.

A second after he was gone the blast of his shotgun tore apart the stillness of the harbor night. In the darkness of the salon Marie Vernon was invisible but not inaudible. The noise coming out of her was somewhere between a long moan and a strangled scream. I was on my hands and knees, feeling my way around her raincoat. As my hand closed on the automatic, the shotgun boomed again outside. Farther away, along the wharf.

I came to my feet and went out the door onto the deck. After the salon it was relatively light outside. I could see Colin sprinting away from the wharf. A moment later he vanished into the maze of the dock facilities. Two men were running after him. I thought I saw the glint of weapons in their hands. But they weren't trying to shoot Colin down. I realized I hadn't heard any shots at all except from Colin's shotgun.

That was curious. But not curious enough for me to stick around there on the barge deck pondering reasons why.

I went down the gangplank and stepped over one of Huang's bodyguards. He was sprawled on his back with one leg dangling over the edge of the wharf. He stared up at me with eyes that somebody else would have to close eventually. His chest was wet pulp. I left him behind and took the wharf's open passageway, holding the automatic ready.

I almost fired it when I caught the gleam of something in a side doorway of the warehouse. The gleam was Huang's rimless spectacles. Huang pressed himself backward and threw up his hands just in time, showing them empty. I grasped the front of his jacket with my free hand and tugged him out of the doorway. "Don't move," I told him.

Huang nodded quickly and I continued past him, moving sidewise so I could keep an eye on him. He stayed the way I'd left him with his empty hands still in the air above his head.

Another of his bodyguards was farther along the passage. He sat leaning against the warehouse wall making thin gasping sounds. He didn't seem to notice me going around his shotgun-smashed legs.

When I was off the wharf, I ran to the Mercedes. I did a fast job of getting into it and out of the harbor area. I didn't want to be around when the cops showed up. It had been a long day and a hard night, and I could do without any more of it.

⊠ **13** ⊠

I SLEPT THE REST OF THAT MORNING AWAY. IT WAS SIX MIN-
utes before noon when Pauline Jacobs phoned my hotel room
and woke me. By the time I'd showered myself half-awake,
the big brunch I had ordered arrived at my room. I phoned
Arlette and Fritz while I drank my second coffee and gave
them what I'd learned so far in Antwerp. I didn't tell Fritz
how to follow up on any of it. He'd been working at our trade
longer than I'd been alive.

The only new information I got from that call was that
Roux had been picked up by the police in Marseilles. As a
result of a tip Fritz had gotten from an underworld contact
and passed on. As we'd expected, Roux flatly denied passing
any message from Colin to Arlette or anyone else. And he
was almost certain to continue swearing to that.

The bigger unsurprising news of the day, from both Paris
and Antwerp, was that Colin was still on the loose somewhere.

Locally, the most interesting bit of no-news concerned the
shooting at the docks around Huang's wharf. The media had
nothing at all on it. Pauline learned from the police that
they'd gone there in response to calls about what sounded
like gunfire. They'd arrived to find nothing at all. What they
hadn't found included any of Huang's bodyguards. Alive or
dead. Huang told the cops he'd heard the noise, too. He

couldn't identify what it was, but he was fairly sure it hadn't been guns.

It was listed in the police blotter as another false alarm.

Pauline had another piece of information for me when I joined her outside my hotel. Marie Vernon had skipped town, according to the woman she shared her apartment with. She had come back there early that morning, packed a suitcase, and left with it. She hadn't said where she was going, except that she was leaving Belgium for a while.

I spent the rest of that afternoon with Pauline in the jewelry industry area around Pelikaanstraat. We met with two gemstone cutters and a diamond merchant. Men that Pauline knew sometimes moonlighted with stolen gems. They knew in turn that nothing they revealed in her presence would get relayed to the law.

None of the three had heard a whisper about the Antibes loot being cut up or fenced. The globe-circling connections between the people who handle precious stones in quantity is closer than family. A dealer from New York can visit the diamond center in Toronto or Tel Aviv and leave with a pouch of baubles worth a fortune, giving nothing for it but his unwritten word it will be paid for later. In a professional world that intimate, lack of any word at all about the Antibes jewels had to mean they weren't circulating anywhere. Not even underground.

It fitted with other indications I'd encountered in Antwerp that one thing Colin had told Arlette might be true: The jewels were still hidden and only Colin knew where.

Unless Christine Boyer did, too.

Pauline Jacobs handed me another dead end just before I drove back to Brussels Airport. Her government and banking sources couldn't turn up a single record of Christine Boyer having lived in Belgium. Not even checks to her from Huang's accountant. Apparently she had worked black—off the books—and Huang had paid her in cash.

There was more of the same waiting for me in Paris that evening. According to Fritz's contacts there were no official documents indicating Christine Boyer had ever been in France. No entry visa, residence permit, work card, or bank account. Nothing.

Another thing I'd gotten in Antwerp was confirmed by Arlette. She had spent most of the day out having very private meetings with Fritz's sources in the Paris gem business. Fritz had sent her out to handle that because his sources were leery about discussing delicate matters over a phone. They told Arlette what I'd been told around Pelikaanstraat. There was nothing trickling through the gem world's grapevine about any of the goods from the Antibes robbery being cut up for illicit sale.

Fritz and Arlette listened without comment when I told them what I'd done between landing in Paris and joining them. A short session with the *juge d'instruction* in charge of the inquiry into André Colin's escape from prison. To give my eyewitness account of the message Roux had delivered to Arlette from Colin. It had been received as anticipated. My statement had been typed up, signed by me, and filed with Roux's conflicting statement. After which the *juge* had reminded me, with a pointedly noncommittal expression, that if my statement proved to be the false one, the charge against me would be perjury. With serious consequences.

I took Fritz and Arlette out to dinner at Julien, one of her favorite Paris restaurants. We concentrated on our meal until our after-dinner drinks. By the time those arrived Fritz was looking and feeling too fatigued for much discussion of what we had and didn't have. At that point, anyway, what we didn't have was a mountain beside the molehill of what we did. And what little we had was mostly unverified surmise.

I drove us home and Fritz went to bed early. Arlette and I weren't fatigued, but once inside my own apartment next door, we went to bed early, too. Going to bed with Arlette was usually a guarantee, after prolonged pleasantries, of a sound sleep with soothing dreams. But the dream that hit me toward the end of that night's sleep was far from soothing.

It was an old dream. I'd had it occasionally in the past, waking up from it in a cold sweat. It held the kind of fear that only childhood knows about, because that was when it had started. Back when I was a kid and staying with my American grandparents in Chicago during school terms. My bedroom in their house had been the room of my dead father whom I'd never known and there were pictures of him on the bureau. I knew the dream grew out of that.

The dream always began with me trudging endlessly between snowdrifts during a near-blizzard night, trying to find my way to someplace safe and warm. The overcoat I wore belonged to my father, stolen out of his bedroom closet. It didn't protect me from the icy wind that made me lurch and stumble between the white drifts.

I was never sure where I was because the scene around me kept shape-shifting—from an empty street under the elevated tracks of the Loop to the middle of a graveyard. Wherever it was, I was lost. And terrified because I knew what was going to happen next.

I was searching for a way out among snowdrifts higher than me when my father climbed out of one of them.

He looked like the last pictures taken of him before he died—a young man of twenty. But he moved like a corpse halfway into rigor mortis. I tried to back away as he came toward me with his stiffened arms jerking open to embrace me. But I couldn't move. Rooted there, I watched him come nearer with his face starting to change into a skull.

That had always been how the dream ended. But not this time. The difference began with the fact that while his face was my father's the chilling smile belonged to Colin. And this time he raised a shotgun and aimed it at me. When he squeezed the trigger, the explosion blew me away and jolted me awake.

I opened my eyes, sitting bolt upright in bed. Morning sunlight streamed through my bedroom blinds, and there was the smell of coffee, and the explosion turned out to be Arlette slamming the bedroom door to wake me.

⊠ 14 ⊠

"SORRY ABOUT THAT." ARLETTE REOPENED THE DOOR BE-hind her. "You were having a nightmare. It seemed the quickest way to break you out of it."

"A kiss would have kinder," I grumbled thickly. The dream was already dissolving and its childhood terror be-longed to someone I hadn't been in touch with for a good many years. There had been too many real dangers to cope with since then.

"I was afraid to come that close," Arlette told me. "You were flailing your fists. And *snarling*—like a wolf about to attack."

She pointed to the large coffee cup she had put on the bedside table and went back out along my apartment corridor to the kitchen. I drank half of my coffee in three long swal-lows. While it cleared my throat and brain I pulled a pillow against the headboard and sat up straighter and looked at the gray weather outside my window. Paris hadn't gotten around to spring yet. But it was pleasantly warm inside, thanks to everyone in the building finally coughing up enough dough for central heating. For which I was grateful. Sleeping in the raw has its advantages, but waking up in a frigid room is not one of them.

I was taking my time with the rest of my coffee when Arlette came back carrying her own cup. She had wrapped my terry cloth bathrobe around her nudity. It reached down to her feet and was much too big for her in every other direction. But it didn't make her any less tantalizing.

Holding her cup carefully, Arlette sat on the bed with me and tucked her feet under her. She studied me as she took a sip of coffee. "You're all right now."

I nodded. "The dream was about Colin—partly."

"No wonder it turned into a nightmare. You're playing games with a highly dangerous, unstable man. That scares me, too. You can't give him Christine because he probably wants to kill her, but if you don't, he may kill you."

"Something about that doesn't make sense," I said. It was as though the dream had clarified my thinking. Or perhaps just the night's sleep, away from Antwerp. "Colin escapes from prison and the first thing he does is go after Christine Boyer. Logically the first thing would be for him to go deep underground. And the second thing—after he waited long enough for the hunt for him to slacken—would be to get those Antibes jewels. If he really has them hidden somewhere. And I think he does."

"I do, too," Arlette said. "That would explain why Colin had to shoot his way past Huang's men in Antwerp—and why they didn't shoot back. They want the jewels and they can't kill him before finding out where he has them."

She looked like she was bothered by another idea of her own, concerned with something I'd said before. But she drank more of her coffee and let me get my thoughts out of my system first.

"My guess," I said, "is that Huang's outfit supplied the other gunmen for the Antibes heist. And Colin double-crossed them. Gave the others the slip and took all the loot with him. Then Huang organized his escape from prison, to get the jewels from him."

"And Colin somehow gave them the slip again."

I scowled at the cup in my hand. "But if that's the way it was, Colin should be taking care of business first. Holing up and waiting out the police dragnets. Then going for the jewels. *Afterward* he could hunt for Christine Boyer. No rush. If all he wants with her is revenge for her telling the cops how to catch him."

Arlette gave me her own thought then: "When it comes to revenge, Colin has a record of wanting it immediately. Remember Gaetan Mora. The one who tipped the police about Colin and the rest of that bank gang. Colin went after Mora while the hunt for him was at its hottest. He doesn't always function on logic alone."

"You've got a point there," I acknowledged. "But it doesn't feel right this time. Colin was *glad* Christine Boyer's still alive somewhere. That nobody killed her."

"Perhaps because he wants to do that himself."

I finished the last of my coffee and set the cup on the table next to the bed. "Have I missed something in his life story? Is there some part of it you forgot to tell us? Has Colin ever killed a woman?"

Arlette considered for a moment. "You may have something. The answer is no, he never has."

"Has he ever *hurt* a woman physically?"

"Not that I know of. But he did threaten to kill Marie Vernon if she lied to him."

"*Threatened.* She's scared of him because he *is* a killer, and I think he used that to bluff her. I think he's got a weird corner in his weird head about women. Maybe because his first kill was to protect his mother. Whatever the crazy reason, it's there."

"You're reaching."

"I know it. But the feeling I get is pretty strong. He's not out to kill Christine."

"Think he loves her?"

"Uh-uh. I don't think he could love a woman any more than he could hurt one. The other side of his kink."

Arlette sipped at her coffee. "Amateur psychoanalysis aside, you figure his being so anxious to find Christine has something to do with those jewels. That she has them or knows where they are. That would explain why Huang had people searching for her."

"Only that doesn't feel right either," I admitted grudgingly. "I can't picture Colin giving her that loot or telling her where he hid it. But—it's still an intriguing notion."

Arlette raised her cup and regarded me over its rim. "I know how your mind works. Deviously, more often than not. What intrigues you is the possibility of our getting hold of those Antibes jewels. Then we wouldn't have to *prove* I didn't help in Colin's escape. You want to get the jewels and hold them back—use them as a lever on the companies that insured them."

"Money and power still talk loudest. Those insurance firms have their cannons loaded with both. They could pound the government into crossing you off its suspect list—if we make them want to badly enough."

"I admit," Arlette said slowly, "that I'd like to be allowed to go back to work at my profession. However it can be accomplished. But . . ."

"But my intriguing notion has too many *ifs*," I said, scowling over them. "*If* Christine Boyer knows where the jewels are. *If* I can get to her before Colin. Or Huang—he'll be hunting her again now he knows that Colin is."

Arlette put her cup aside and smiled and soothed my brow with deft, tender fingertips. "Stop battering your poor old brain for a while, Pierre-Ange. Give it a rest."

I came out of my dark thoughts and focused on her dark eyes. After a moment I said, "Good thought."

I opened the bathrobe she was wearing and slid my hands

in under it. Her smile changed in mysterious ways as she let the pressure of my hand on the small of her back bring her closer. The feel of her against me brought the surge of passion it always did. I kissed her and she moved her shoulders and the bathrobe slipped away. Her lips were sweeter than any ripe fruit and much more mobile.

That's when her father knocked on my apartment door.

⊠ **15** ⊠

I DIDN'T KNOW IT WAS HER FATHER WHEN I TRAIPSED OUT of the bedroom bare-assed. The most likely visitor at that hour of the morning was Fritz, coming over from the next apartment to have breakfast with us. I did pick up a large towel from the bathroom before continuing along the apartment's corridor. I knotted it around my waist as I crossed my living room and asked who was there.

Marcel Alfani identified himself through the locked door.

There was nothing to do but unlock it and let him in. I hoped like hell Arlette had the good sense to stay out of sight in the bedroom. Or at least get fully dressed before coming out. Marcel Alfani had begun his climb up the underworld ladder as a sixteen-year-old pimp. But where his own family was concerned he had never relinquished the strict Corsican morality of his island birthplace.

There were two much younger men standing in the hallway behind him. Bodyguards. I remembered one of them from before. The other was new. They looked like brothers. Big shoulders, swarthy expressionless faces, sport jackets loose enough on them so the hardware underneath wouldn't show.

In contrast with them Alfani looked like a retired professor. He had since I'd known him, with that short white beard and those black-framed glasses. But that impression was more definite now. Since he'd had half his stomach removed because of a bleeding ulcer, he had lost much of the muscle that had helped him fight his way to the top of his chosen profession. He still held himself tall, however. And the dark eyes behind those glasses still showed the harsh intelligence and quiet menace that had made him the reigning gangster in Southern France for two decades.

"Come in," I said. There was no way to keep him out.

He stepped inside and shut the door, leaving his boys outside. He looked around the living room and then at me and my towel. "Isn't Arlette here? Your partner said she might be."

Thanks a lot, Fritz.

I said, "I thought you were off visiting some old pal in California."

"I was. Then somebody got word to me, about this trouble Arlette's got herself into."

"She didn't get herself into it, Marcel. Dédé Colin suckered her into it."

"Whatever. I came back to help get her out of it." His attention abruptly swung away from me—to Arlette.

She came into the living room wearing a cheery smile and my bathrobe. I sighed inwardly. Alfani watched her approach with a hard stare.

His hard stares never flustered Arlette. She kissed him and patted his cheek. "You look better, Papa. That California climate did you good."

Marcel Alfani switched his hard stare to me. Unlike Arlette, I was not unmoved by it. "I'll wait for you on the *place*," he told me. "In one of those bistros. We got to talk."

"I'll be down," I promised.

He turned around and walked out.

Place Contrescarpe was half a block from the house where Fritz and I had our apartments. There were four scraggly trees growing from the raised pedestrian section in the middle of it. There were two clochards and a dog sleeping between one of the trees and an emptied wine bottle. There was Marcel Alfani waiting for me in the glassed-in terrace of one of Contrescarpe's four bistros, with his bodyguards at the next table to fend off unwanted company.

I ordered an *express* from the bar in passing and sat down across the table from him. He was nursing an herb tea. The doctors had forbidden him caffeine and he'd never cared much for liquor.

He listened attentively while I filled him in on the details of Arlette's problem. When I finished, he said, "What kind of help can I give you?"

"Two things," I told him. "First, there's a man named Huang Yok Lin. Ever heard of him?"

Marcel Alfani shook his head. "Chinese?"

"Yes, but from Thailand. He's involved in importing illegal immigrants. Probably other underground activities as well. In Antwerp. But he used to be here in Paris and maybe he still has operations going here. He owns an import-export firm up there called HYL-Orient Trading Company. I'd like to know anything more you can find out about him."

"I'll ask around," Marcel Alfani said. "Some people I still know from the old days."

"The second thing involves protecting Arlette. Colin knows I'm working for her, and Huang will have found out by now. One or the other of them could get a notion to stop something I might be doing by grabbing her." I jerked a thumb at the two bodyguards. "Can you get some more like those?"

I was pretty sure Arlette would go along with the need for that kind of precaution. She wasn't a fearful person, but not careless either.

Her father nodded. "As many as you need."

"I'd like a few to keep an eye on my place all the time, to make sure nobody who looks like a threat gets in there at her. And a couple of them ought to trail her around whenever she goes out.''

Marcel Alfani got that hard menace back in his stare. "You admit it. She's staying with you. Nights, too."

"Marcel, you know Arlette and I have been seeing a lot of each other. It can't be a sudden shock to you."

The stare didn't change at all. "Are you going to get around to marrying her one of these days, or not?''

He didn't ask if Arlette was going to get around to marrying me. Women's liberation was an event Marcel Alfani had never noticed.

"That," I told him quietly and firmly, "is none of your business at this point, Marcel."

His eyes stayed riveted to mine and they didn't soften. He drew a soft breath and I saw veins bulge in his temples. But when he spoke again, his tone was almost gentle: "I knew your mother back when you were still inside her. Maybe that's why I've always liked you. I hope I don't have to stop feeling that way about you."

I wondered, not for the first time, if it was too late for me to fall in love with someone other than Marcel Alfani's daughter.

⊠ **16** ⊠

I PARKED MY RENAULT 5 NEAR THE INTERNATIONAL BANK of China and walked through the heart of Paris's thirteenth arrondissement. It was lined with shops and restaurants and swarming with people going briskly about their own businesses. Laotians, Malays, Cambodians, Vietnamese, Indonesians, Chinese, Koreans. Europeans, too, but they were a conspicuous minority in this densely populated quarter.

Parisians call the thirteenth arrondissement Chinatown-on-the-Seine. Some of the Indochinese refugees who live there reverse the geographical image and refer to it as Paris-on-the-Mekong. Except for the abundance of Oriental signs and people it could have been a reconstructed neighborhood in any part of the Western world. Most of the old buildings had been leveled and replaced by malls and open squares surrounded by tall, massed apartment and business complexes. That didn't lessen the hermetic character of its polyglot Asian community, wrapped in an enigmatic, invisible camouflage.

I turned into one of the few old streets that the demolition cranes hadn't gotten to yet. A narrow, cobbled dead-end street of dilapidated two- and four-floor houses. It had only recently become Oriental, as thousands fleeing the revolutions and counterrevolutions of Southeast Asia squeezed into Paris's Chinatown and pushed its boundaries outward.

The herbal store of Lu Tse-sing had been a kosher butcher shop in the past. On the outside wall parts of faded Hebrew letters still showed under the new sign painted in Chinese.

The interior had a dozen customers being waited on by a stocky woman and a slim girl of about twelve. The odor of spices and seaweed tickled the nostrils. Dozens of open bins contained roots and powders, dried fruits and kelp, seeds and teas. On the shelves around the walls packaged remedies from homeopathic firms were outnumbered by jars of Lu Tse-sing's own concoctions.

Everyone looked my way when I entered. They didn't get many Occidentals here. The stocky woman said something to a customer and came over to me. "Can I help you?"

"Is Dr. Lu around?" I asked, and told her my name.

"Ah—you are Monsieur Donhoff's friend."

"If you are Dr. Lu's wife," I said, "Monsieur Donhoff asked me to tell you that he still lusts for you."

Lust was the word Fritz had insisted on.

She dimpled prettily when she smiled. "I *am* the wife of Dr. Lu. That Monsieur Donhoff—all men should grow old with his childish delight in life."

Her French was still halting though she'd been in Paris for years. Since she and her husband had escaped from China during its "cultural revolution"—when teenage hoodlums had been officially encouraged to harass and beat "intellectuals."

"Just a moment," she said. "My daughter will take you to the doctor." She left me and spoke softly to the young girl.

Her daughter came over to me with a friendly, open smile. "Papa said to expect you. Come with me, please." Her French was like that of any schoolkid born in the country. She wore the usual outfit of her age group. Raggedy jeans and a sweatshirt three sizes too big for her. The sweatshirt was purple. It had KEEP COOL printed across the front in bright yellow. No self-respecting kid in France would be caught dead wearing one with anything French on it. Turning out the fake American stuff is a big money-maker for the nation's clothing industry.

I followed her through a back door into a storage room where the air was thick with a peppery dust that almost made me sneeze. We went out of that into a little courtyard and up a covered stairway to a room on the second floor. People who looked like everything from Tibetans to Filipinos sat on benches against two walls. Patients waiting their turn with the doctor.

"Stay here a moment, please," the girl told me. She opened a door and shut it behind her as she went through into the next room. I stood there and smiled at the people on the benches. Most of them smiled back politely. The couple who didn't were obviously in too much pain to.

Lu Tse-sing didn't have any legal right to practice medicine in France. His patients didn't care about that. They knew he was as good a doctor here as he'd been in China. The inspectors over at the police commissariat on Boulevard de l'Hôpital would have cared. If they had known what he was doing in their arrondissement. But they didn't know. For the same reason that they hadn't been able to give me or Fritz any of the information we were after.

The Far Eastern community of the thirteenth was a closed world filled with whispers that seldom leaked out.

The cops had been working four years on a mass killing in one of the area's apartment towers. All they had so far was what they'd had the first day of their investigation. The victims had all been Cambodian refugees from the Pol Pot era, so the motive was probably but not surely political vengeance. And the police still didn't have a clue to the identities of six young Oriental women who'd been turned up by a bulldozer from under a communal garden—where they'd been buried over a period of years by an unknown murderer for unknown reasons.

You needed somebody inside this society to find out what was going on under its gentle surface bustle.

Dr. Lu's daughter reappeared and motioned to me. I went through into a simple examination room and she closed the door from the other side.

Dr. Lu was fiddling with a small machine attached to a set of batteries. He was a short man in his sixties, as slim as his daughter, with sparse gray hair, a deeply wrinkled face, and pensive eyes. "Just a minute longer, Monsieur Sawyer," he said, giving me a brief smile. "I am almost through with this patient." His smile was boyish, making you forget the wrinkles.

His patient was a burly man in his forties. He sat on the examination table with his legs extended and his trousers rolled up to his knees. An acupuncture needle was stuck into each of his ankles. Electric wires ran from the needles to the machine and batteries.

"One last time," Dr. Lu told the man, speaking in French. The population of Chinatown comprised so many utterly different language groups, they needed French to communicate with one another.

The patient gripped the side of the examination table and braced himself. There was a small buzzing noise from the machine as Dr. Lu switched it on. His patient made a sound that was half pleasure and half stifled alarm as the mild electric charge hit him. After about twenty seconds Dr. Lu switched off the current. "That will help," he said while carefully removing the needles from the man's ankles. "I will give you a longer dose of it on your next visit."

His patient rolled down his trousers and paid for his treatment in cash. They bowed to each other before the man left.

"I do what I can," Dr. Lu sighed after closing the door. "Impotence and the fear of it—such a common complaint. What can I tell the poor man—and his poor wife? That they have been married for over twenty years and a little variety might be a further aid in perking him up? His wife is too modern to accept that, and he is too devoted a husband to offend her. The attempt would only make him more tense and defeat its purpose. As well as harming an excellent marriage.''

''You mean it's all in his head.''

Dr. Lu detached one needle from its wire and put it carefully into a tall jar filled with alcohol. ''The mental and physical are not two separate things, Monsieur Sawyer. The nerves are part of the body and the brain is part of the nervous system. Acupuncture with an electrical charge does sometimes help to relieve the problem.''

He put the other needle into the jar and suddenly gave me another boyish smile. ''I also gave him some powdered rhinoceros horn.''

''Genuine?''

''Of course not. Rhino horn has become too rare and expensive. There won't be any rhinos left alive soon, except a few in zoos. Too many people using it to restore virility. But the patient who just left believes what I gave him is genuine, so it may work for him. We'll see.'' Another quick smile. ''A bit of charlatanism is sometimes called for in my profession.''

He went to a corner sink to wash his hands. ''How is my old friend Fritz coming along?''

''Slowly. He still gets tired too quickly. That's why he didn't come here to see you himself. I'm doing the running around for him.''

''Have my wife give you my mixture of honey and iodine when you leave. Tell Fritz to take two large spoonfuls of it twice each day. Half an hour before meals. Within a few weeks he should feel a renewal of energy.''

Dr. Lu dried his hands and sat on the edge of his desk. ''Now, then, how can I help you and Fritz?''

''We're looking for a young woman named Christine Boyer. About twenty years old now. She's half Vietnamese but she looks entirely European. Blue eyes, light brown hair. Pretty.''

Dr. Lu thought about it and shook his head. "I don't know her. Nor have I ever heard the name."

"She came to Paris from Vietnam," I told him. "But there's no record of her having been here. That means she got in illegally."

"Not unusual. As an educated guess, I would estimate that almost half the recent Oriental population of Paris consists of illegals."

"Brought here from the East by underworld networks with the means for transporting people by underground routes," I said. "One of those networks must have smuggled Christine Boyer in. If I can learn which one, it may help me locate her."

"There are a number of criminal groups involved in smuggling people. The largest, I believe, is based in Singapore with branches in Thailand and Europe as well. A triad called the Association of the Thin Blade. Its fighters are reputed to be exceptionally fierce."

"I've picked up rumors about another triad supposed to be involved in people smuggling," I said. "The Red Lotus Society—with its roots in Hong Kong."

"I have heard the name," Dr. Lu told me. "Beyond that I know nothing concerning it. I can make some inquiries. But only with extreme discretion. These people smugglers are as dangerous as they are secretive."

"They've got a big source of income to protect. I don't know how most of the illegals raise the small fortune the smugglers charge each one."

"With great difficulty—in any way they can. Often the ways are long and disgusting. And once they are over here they are often victimized by the very gangs that brought them in. Extortion—they are so vulnerable to that, coming in without a valid visa. These gangs can continue to control them for years. Force them to work at one job and not another, for example. Take part of everything they earn.''

"I know. They have a hard life.''

"But not as hard as the life they escaped from," Dr. Lu added, from his own experience. "And here at least they have hope. For the future of their families. Their children, born here, are automatically legal citizens. These illegals are prepared to sacrifice their own generation to that end.''

"Do you know of a man named Huang Yok Lin?" I asked him.

He thought longer over this name. "It is a name I have heard before. Somewhere in the past. But I can't remember in what connection.''

"He came here from Thailand. Probably Bangkok. He owns a place in Antwerp named the Bangkok Bar.'' I watched Dr. Lu as I came up with each point about Huang. "He also owns an import-export firm up there. HYL-Orient.''

But none of it reestablished the connection for him. "Perhaps it was too long ago for me to remember. Or it was some other name like this one.''

"Huang is also associated with an operation bringing people into Europe from the East illegally. I'm almost certain his outfit is the one that brought Christine Boyer over. She knew him here and she worked for him in the Antwerp bar.''

"That is quite possible,'' Dr. Lu said. "Since you say this Huang is from Thailand and the girl from Vietnam. Most people escaping from Vietnam would escape into Thailand first.''

"While you're asking around about Christine Boyer, please check for me on Huang Yok Lin. And on which smuggling ring might be connected to both.''

Lu Tse-sing nodded. "I will call Fritz if I learn anything. But I don't care to say too much over a phone.''

"Just tell Fritz you have something of interest. I'll come around and get the rest from you.''

And that was that. I'd done what I'd come for. Spreading

the word. I had done the same through most of yesterday and I would do more of it this afternoon. Seeing Fritz's contacts—and a couple of my own—in Chinatown-on-the-Seine. Telling each what I was after and asking all of them to check around. Spreading the word is more than fifty percent of the brute labor in most investigations. Ask enough of the right people questions and eventually you might start getting answers. There's an element of luck in it, too—but you've got to push it in the right direction.

Dr. Lu Tse-sing smiled and shook my hand as he opened the door for me to leave. His smile wasn't boyish this time. It was an old man's smile. I had made him think too much about parts of his life that he would prefer to forget.

I picked up Fritz's medicine from Dr. Lu's wife on the way out and continued my Chinatown prowl, looking for the linked pasts of Christine Boyer and Huang Yok Lin.

The method might have seemed haphazard to an outsider. But it was much like the work of search-and-rescue teams combing back and forth through a forest in search of plane crash survivors. If they're working the right area, the odds are on their side.

I was sure our team was working the right areas. Fritz and Arlette over their phones, me legging it around Chinatown, Alfani in his underworld circles, and Pauline Jacobs up in Belgium. Time was the chancy factor now. If it didn't run out on us, one of our team was bound to come across tracks somebody had left behind in this forest.

It began happening the following day.

⊠ **17** ⊠

I DROVE PAST THE WHITE HOUSE THE NEXT AFTERNOON AND parked near the Kremlin.

Some Parisians claim that putting those two stations that close together, on the same Métro line with no other station between them, was France's contribution to ending the Cold War. Back in more hopeful days. Before The Wall changed the Iron Curtain into solid fact.

There is no Iron Curtain separating *La Maison Blanche* and *Le Kremlin-Bicêtre* in Paris. What does lie between them is a vast cemetery with thousands of graves. The bistro philosophers of that quarter find that apt. They see the cemetery as the future of Europe if those Métro stations quit snarling and start shooting.

Lee To Hyun's place was a couple blocks from the Kremlin station. An old but well-cared-for brick and stucco three-story house with a slanting tin roof, squeezed between a plastics factory and a tire distributor's warehouse. Inside Lee's house you heard the vibration of sewing machines wherever you were. At least fifty of them—operated at high speed by Oriental women ranging in age from about eleven years old into their seventies.

"I admit," Lee said after leading me past some of them into his tiny office, "that I run what Americans would call a sweatshop. But I do pay my employees—as much as I can and still sell the clothing they make for less than normal companies charge. So I cannot pay them normal wages. Does that mean I exploit them? I don't think so. None of these people have proper work papers. Most do not have permits to live in France. If I did not employ them, they would starve. Does that make me a dirty boss—or a benefactor?"

"It's Christine Boyer I came to talk about," I reminded him. "I'm not qualified to judge the state of your soul."

"I know." Lee To Hyun's smile was apologetic. "It's simply nerves. I rattle on about nothing sometimes when I'm nervous."

"No reason to be—not with me."

"Dr. Lu assures me of that. He tells me that nothing I reveal to you will be used to harm me—or Christine."

"You have my assurance on that, too," I told him.

"But I don't know you, Monsieur Sawyer. I do know Dr. Lu—and trust him." Lee smiled again to take any sting out of that.

He was a solidly built, handsome man of about thirty-six with a lot of striking contradictions to him. The skin color and most of the bone structure of his face were as distinctly Oriental as the epicanthic fold in his upper eyelids. But there was nothing Oriental about the blue of his eyes or the hawk-like nose. He had strong shoulders and large hands that looked like they would make efficient fists. But I didn't detect any latent aggression in him. He had the expression of a habitually agreeable man. And for a businessman his attire was definitely antiestablishment. Unzippered red windbreaker over a plaid wool shirt, jeans tucked into scuffed cowboy boots.

I told him: "There are two men searching for Christine Boyer. One is a psychopathic killer. The other is a gangster. If I can find her before either of those men, I can protect her from them."

"Yes—you do look capable of doing so." Lee nodded over that, continuing to study me for several moments. Then he relaxed a bit and said, "If Christine is in trouble, I certainly want to help her in any way I can. I have an affinity with Christine. Our lives have been very different, but our origins were so alike." Lee gestured at his blue eyes. "As you can see."

"Dr. Lu said you're from South Korea."

"Yes—I was born in the port city of Pusan. In 1952. During the war of the United Nations forces and South Koreans against the Chinese and North Koreans. My mother was Korean, my father an American soldier. He said he intended to marry her—or so she always claimed. But when she was five months pregnant with me he went away and never came back. I choose to believe he was killed in battle, rather than that he deliberately deserted us. Since I never knew him, I can never be sure what sort of man he was."

I wondered if Lee To Hyun ever had unpleasant dreams in which he met his stranger-father. But I wasn't there for an exchange of childhood traumas. "There's an important difference between you and Christine Boyer," I said. "Nobody would miss the fact you're part Oriental. I'm told that she looks entirely Occidental."

"True. But that didn't make the problem she shared with me any easier—as long as she lived in the East. Back there we were both what they call half persons. Neither Oriental nor Occidental. Cut off from each by the other half of us. Accepted by no group. That was what drew me to Christine so strongly when I first met her."

"Where was that?"

"In the middle of the Gulf of Thailand," Lee answered. "Halfway between Thailand and Vietnam. When she was thirteen. I had left Korea long before that."

"Political exile?"

Lee laughed and shook his head. "I wish I could claim such high-minded motives. But no—I left for a more mundane reason. I had come to realize, finally, that no self-respecting family was going to allow its daughter to marry a half person. So I raised the money to get out." He hesitated, and then went on with it: "The means I used to raise enough money were for the most part criminal. Stealing from cargos around the port. Selling smuggled goods on the black market. Does that shock you, Monsieur Sawyer?"

"When a man's up against the wall, he does what he has to in order to survive. Within limits, if he's got a conscience."

Lee regarded me with approval. "I see that you, too, have lived a life of ups and downs."

"Which makes some transgressions of the law unavoidable," I admitted. "I always try to transgress as delicately as possible, of course."

He laughed again. We were buddies now. "I found it necessary to continue my transgressions in the next country I went to. Thailand. Because I found my personal situation no better there. I was still a half person. I decided to move on to Europe—where things *are* better. But I didn't want to come here as a pauper. So—a little smuggling across the Thai-Burmese border."

"Heroin?"

"No—I do draw the line against certain acts against humanity, Monsieur Sawyer. There are commodities one can handle without harming others. Tools and plumbing supplies and medicines smuggled into Burma, for example. Rubies and jade and works of religious art smuggled out of Burma. But it was dangerous work. Large underworld syndicates control most of the smuggling along that border. They enjoy inflicting gruesome deaths on independents. I didn't have the courage to continue running that risk for too long."

"I'd say you were braver than most to try it at all," I said—and figured I'd buttered him up enough by then to get him to the point: "About Christine Boyer . . ."

"I met her during a different kind of smuggling venture," he told me. "A Vietnamese fishing boat was due to slip out at night from the coast near Rach Gia with ancient art treasures concealed in its hold. Objects looted inside Vietnam. Buddha heads, manuscripts, ceremonial tea bowls, carved jade. Several other men and I put together enough money to buy it all. The price to us was thirty times less than what we could sell it for after we transported it to Europe.

"We rented a boat at Pak Phanang, on the southeast coast of Thailand, and sailed out to meet the one from Vietnam. Our rendezvous point was to be off an empty rock of an island called Koh Kra. When we neared it, we used binoculars and saw there what could be the fishing vessel with its concealed treasure. But there were two smaller fishing boats hooked onto it. Pirates from those had boarded the larger boat. We could see them stripping people on its deck, throwing some overboard, raping women.

"When we closed in on them, the pirates jumped back into their own boats and raced away. We were well armed, and they were not. One had a revolver, another had an old rifle, and the rest only knives or short swords. They were only poor Thai fishermen, turning to piracy to add to their meager incomes."

"And," I put in, "not averse to adding rape and murder to robbery, just for the hell of it."

"There are some men, Monsieur Sawyer, who drop *all* normal restraints once they take that first step and transgress."

"Too damn many. In the Thailand Gulf and the streets of any American city."

Lee To Hyun nodded, sighed helplessly, and continued his story. "We didn't find our treasure on that boat. All it had been carrying was refugees from Vietnam desperately trying to escape to Thailand. Only eight of them were left alive—an old man, a baby, and six young women. The pirates planned to sell the females to brothels. The youngest of them was Christine.

"She had been raped by each of the nine pirates. She was

very pretty and looked European—an unusual toy for their amusement, I suppose. They had cut her mother's throat when she tried to interfere. Christine had nobody left. And she was in very bad condition at first.''

Lee shook his head admiringly. ''But even then, she had such *determination* in her. Her French was rudimentary at that time, but sufficient for us to converse. We spoke with each other a great deal as she regained strength in the two days we waited for our boatload of treasure to arrive. It never did, by the way. Perhaps other pirates got it. Or it leaked and foundered on the way. Or it never left Vietnam.

''But Christine—she fascinated me. Because of the kinship between us. And the strength of her spirit. For her, Thailand was only a first step. She was determined to get to Europe. For the same reason as I—to reach a place where she could *belong*. But her fixity of purpose was even stronger than mine.''

''What was her real name?'' I asked Lee.

''Tran So Lan. But she was already insisting on using the Western name she'd chosen for herself. Boyer, because her mother had told her that was her father's family name. Christine, that was just a name she had picked up somewhere. Christine Boyer—with the family name last, in the Western manner.

''We returned to Thailand with her and the other survivors. Except for the baby. One of the pirates had thrown it against a bulkhead when they killed its parents. The injury was fatal. The baby died in Christine's arms. I can never forget the way she watched us drop it into the sea. No tears. What was in her eyes was much more terrible than that. No child of thirteen should look like that.''

Lee To Hyun fell silent and his own eyes became difficult to look at. I'd heard stories as bad before, in Europe and America, told by exiles from all parts of the world. No matter how many you know, you hear each new one feeling like a nail is being driven into your gut. And knowing that nail is nothing compared to what those telling it went through.

I said, "What happened to her in Thailand?"

"She was put into the Phanat Nikhom refugee center. I would have liked to keep her with me, but that was impossible. I lived the life of a bachelor—and a criminal. And I had to be away most of the time, recouping what I lost on that venture in the Thailand Gulf via further trips across the Thai-Burmese border. I visited Christine at Phanat Nikhom after one of those trips. She was healthier, and prettier. But the camp directors were not optimistic about her future.

"She had no identity papers. Her mother had carried those, and the pirates had thrown them into the sea with her after killing her. And it was Thai policy at that period to refuse entry visas, passports, or any other identity papers to Vietnamese refugees—to stem the flood of them pouring into their country. That made Christine a stateless person. She didn't belong to Thailand, she had no papers from Vietnam, and her chances of being legally admitted into any nation in the West were null.

"The next time I went to see her she was gone. The records kept by the refugee camps are not the best. No one could tell me if she had been sent elsewhere. Or had run away from the camp. Or had been taken away—by one of the child-catcher gangs that sell boys and girls to massage parlors and brothels. I searched but couldn't find her.

"The next time I saw Christine she was seventeen."

"Where?"

"Here—in Paris."

◨ **18** ◨

"I WAS OVER IN THE SENTIER QUARTER THAT AFTERNOON," Lee To Hyun said. "Seeing some of my customers in the garment district. I came out of a building on the Rue d'Aboukir and we almost walked into each other. I didn't realize who she was at first. She had changed so much—from a pretty child into a lovely young woman. But she recognized me immediately—and threw her arms around me and kissed me. And after we had hugged each other—and cried a little— I took her to a local brasserie for coffee.

"Christine had just been coming from having lunch with a man in the best restaurant in that neighborhood. She told me she had met him at a party and he claimed to have fallen in love and wanted her to be his mistress. It happens I knew this man. A garment manufacturer. In his fifties. He was notorious for philandering—brief flings with young, naive women.

"I warned her that he was much too old for her and that his protestations of love were false. Christine said she knew it, but that she'd never been to such a top restaurant before and just couldn't resist the opportunity. She laughed and said a good free lunch was a good free lunch, but that she had no intention of becoming his mistress. I realized suddenly," Lee added after a moment, "that I had never seen Christine smile before, let alone laugh."

"Did she tell you how she got from Thailand to France?" I asked him.

"A bit. I only had half an hour with her before I had to be at my next meeting. She said it began with her running away from that refugee camp. She made her way to Bangkok, though she was close to starvation by the time she finished the trip. And once there, she was seized by one of the gangs that hang around the railroad station waiting for kids like her.

"She was luckier than most. They didn't sell her into a brothel. Because her European look made her an amusing oddity they figured they could get more for her elsewhere. They sold her to a Japanese businessman who divided his time between Japan and Thailand. He kept a harem of very young girls in his Bangkok home and he was delighted to add one as interesting-looking as Christine to that harem."

"Better than having to service twenty to thirty men every day," I said.

Lee nodded agreement. "And Christine said he was a kind, gentle man. And with so many girls in the house he made few demands on any one of them. He was so nice to them, she said, that she still felt somewhat guilty about stealing money from him when she was fifteen. Enough money to pay a smuggling ring to transport her to Europe."

"Did she tell you anything about this smuggling ring?"

"No. I assume it is one of the triads."

"Why?"

"Because when Christine arrived in Paris with a group of other illegals—all of them supplied with false passports and entry permits—they were met by a Chinese racketeer associated with the smuggling ring. He—"

"What was his name?" I interrupted.

"Christine didn't tell me that," Lee said.

"Ever heard of one called Huang Yok Lin?"

Lee considered the name before shaking his head. "No.

Is that the man who took charge of Christine and the others when they arrived here?''

"Probably. Almost certainly."

"Whoever he is, he dictated their lives from then on. Warned them that if they ever disobeyed him, the police would be informed their papers were false. That would result in their being shipped back where they came from. Christine told me the room she lived in—and paid exorbitant rent for—was in a building owned by this man's underworld syndicate. And most of the jobs she took were ones to which she was sent by this gangster's underlings—and for which she had to pay them part of her weekly earnings."

I glanced briefly at Lee's office door, through which came the hum of all those sewing machines. Maybe I let some of what I thought show in my expression.

Lee grimaced unhappily. "I know—*I* am in no position to be indignant about the victimizing of illegal refugees. You are right—many of my own employees are supplied to me by similiar syndicates."

"They have to work somewhere," I said, "or starve, as you pointed out earlier. You didn't originate the situation they're in."

"I tell myself that," Lee said. "And I tell myself I can't solve the misery of all the people in this world. I can, however, sometimes help one person at a time."

"You thought of helping Christine Boyer."

"I had an idea just before we parted. If I adopted her, she could become a legal French citizen. Then this gangster and his organization couldn't cause her trouble."

"Or you could have married her," I said. "That would have achieved the same objective."

"Perhaps I did care for her enough to have suggested that," Lee acknowledged. "Except that I was already married. I have three children, and no desire to be an absent father. So adoption was the only possible alternative."

"How did she take the idea?"

"I didn't suggest it. I needed time to think it over. And to discuss it with my wife first. I did tell Christine I had a notion I wanted to discuss with her at another time. I suggested I take her to dinner the following evening. But she said she was going to be away for the rest of the week. Working as a temporary waitress just outside Paris somewhere. She said she would phone me after she came back."

Lee's tone told me the punchline: "But she didn't."

He shook his head. "We kissed each other tenderly when we parted—and I never saw her again."

I thought some about the timing of their meeting. It had to be not long before Huang moved Christine Boyer up to Antwerp.

"Where was she living in Paris?" I asked Lee.

"I have no idea. She wouldn't give me the address and none of the rooms she and the other illegals in that house lived in had telephones."

"Do you know any of the places where she worked?"

"No, I know nothing about Christine's life at that time other than what I have already told you."

"The man she had lunch with that day might know more," I said. "What's his name and where do I find him?"

I watched Lee's guard come up. After a moment he said, "I would have to speak to him first. Before involving him. To find out if he is willing to speak to you about Christine."

"Dr. Lu told you I'm safe," I reminded him.

"He told *me*, yes, but not this man. Who is a Frenchman, not an Oriental. Dr. Lu's recommendation would mean nothing to him. I can't think of any reason he wouldn't want to speak to you about Christine—but I have to ask him first. That is only right. A man is entitled to his privacy if he doesn't wish to be disturbed."

Lee was troubled by his refusal to be more helpful, but stubborn, too. I sensed I couldn't push him. I gestured at the phone on his desk. "Call him and ask. I'll step outside with the sewing machine ladies while you do."

"He doesn't have a phone anymore," Lee told me. "His business went bankrupt a year ago. The unfortunate man is down to pushing clothes racks around the garment district for different firms. And the phone was removed from his apartment because he didn't pay the bill."

"Ran into hard luck."

"Yes—that is another reason I don't want to offend the poor man by sending you to him without his permission. I'll go see him and ask if he wants to meet with you."

"When?"

"Tonight—if he is at home. Otherwise as soon as I can. I'll phone you after I talk to him. I'm sorry, Monsieur Sawyer, but that is the best I can manage for you."

"It will have to do," I said, and gave him Fritz's number and my own. Shoving him would anger Dr. Lu and lose Fritz a good contact. I figured I could get around to more devious methods of locating the hard-luck garment manufacturer later, if his reply turned out to be negative.

I thought about Christine Boyer while I drove away from Lee's place. Her and the life that fate had slammed her with. It was hard to think of anything else for a while. She had become too real for me.

You can't let every personal tragedy you come across get inside your skin. In my line of work there're too many of them. You'd wind up so loaded with rage, you couldn't function efficiently. But now and then one case breaks through the armor.

I made myself cool down. But it took concentration. Between that and avoiding collisions with blind or crazy Parisian drivers I didn't give anything else much attention. It wasn't until I was back on foot inside Chinatown that I sensed I was being followed.

◙ **19** ◙

I HAD BEEN CHECKING FOR A TAIL AT IRREGULAR INTERVALS throughout that day. But this time I checked more carefully. Entering a supermarket and then doubling back out of it. I couldn't spot anybody among the people moving around behind me who seemed interested in my movements—nor anyone suddenly pretending not to be.

Five minutes later I checked again—going into one end of a parking garage and out the other end, turning into an alley and then stopping to watch my back trail. Nothing. But the feeling of being shadowed stayed strong. And I've learned to trust that feeling. It's not always right, but a long time ago I ignored it with painful results.

If you can't spot 'em, shake 'em. I did enough fast and fancy moving around after that to make certain that if there was a tail on me, I had lost it. Then I used a public phone booth to call Fritz's apartment and check in.

It was Arlette who answered the phone. She told me Fritz was taking a nap.

"Any other news at your end?" I asked her.

"Our old friend phoned an hour ago."

We had agreed that it would be safest to refer to André Colin as "old friend" when using our own phones. Arlette was already suspected of complicity in his escape. Any branch of the police following through on that would know

where she was by now and could have our phone lines tapped.
The one thing we couldn't afford to let them hear was evidence that we knew anything about Colin's movements and
hadn't divulged it immediately to the law. That would finish
Arlette's hope of ever practicing her profession again.

I gave her the phone number in my booth. She hung up
and I waited for her to get to a public payphone. There were
nine of them in bistros within a two-block radius of my building for her to choose from.

When she called me back from one of them three minutes
later, I asked her, "Was he calling long-distance—or is he
in Paris?"

"I asked and he didn't answer. He could have been in this
very phone booth for all I could tell. He was surprised when
I took his call, but then he laughed and said it was nice
talking to me again. He was bright enough to not give his
name. Just asked if I recognized his voice."

"What did he want?"

"To find out if you're making progress on finding Christine," Arlette said. "I told him you're working on it. He said
to remind you he's working on it, too. And that if he gets to
her before you do, he won't have to honor his agreement to
get me off the hook."

That wasn't news. And Colin hadn't told Arlette anything
else before he'd hung up. I left my booth considering two
possibly related probables. Colin might be here in Paris—
and that feeling that somebody very good at keeping out of
sight had been tailing me might be correct.

I decided to have another short talk with Marcel Alfani.

When he was in Paris, he always stayed at the Grand Hotel
across from the Opera. That was where he'd stayed the first
time he'd come up from the south with enough ill-gotten cash
in his pockets to splurge on luxury. Marcel Alfani had been
nineteen at that time. The hotel's Café de la Paix hadn't

changed much since then and that was where I spotted him when I walked past its glass wall.

He was at one of the tables with two equally elderly gentlemen, dressed like him in somber, expensive business suits. His bodyguards—and theirs—took up the tables on either side of them.

In the past, Alfani had waged some fairly ferocious underworld battles against each of the men at his table. But they were as retired as he was now—enough to get by these days with only two bodyguards apiece. The three of them were laughing as they talked. Probably recalling what they'd done and tried to do to one another back in the good old days.

I went on into the hotel lobby and used a house phone to have him paged. When he took my call, I told him I'd wait for him outside his suite.

It was on the fourth floor. I was in the corridor outside it when Alfani came out of the elevator with his pair of watchdogs. One of them unlocked the door to his suite and went in to check out its rooms. Then we entered the living room, and Alfani motioned for his boys to disappear into another part of the suite.

When we were alone, he told me, "I haven't got anything at all on that Huang character yet, if that's what you came for."

His manner with me this day was kindly verging on solicitous. Arlette had accomplished the transformation by confiding to him that she was thinking of dropping me but didn't want me to know until she found a way to break it gently. Now Alfani felt sorry for me. And somewhat responsible because it was his daughter who was preparing to break my heart.

"The problem is," he said, "those gangs that've been coming in from the Far East don't mix at all with any of the European businessmen I know. But the word's out I got an interest. Something'll come through. We just got to be patient."

"I think I was being shadowed part of today," I told him. I didn't think the tail had picked me up again when I'd driven over here, but I couldn't be certain. A car tail has become harder to spot than it used to be. Different makes of cars have lost their individuality. A Peugeot looks like a Fiat, which looks like a Honda, Renault, or Volkswagen. In heavy traffic that makes it difficult to impossible to tell if one of the cars behind you is the same one that was back there before you made a few precautionary turns.

"The tail could be Dédé Colin," I added. "If he could be ambushed and taken, I think I can find a way to persuade him to clear Arlette."

"I'll be glad to help with the persuading," Alfani said darkly. "I know some boys that're experts at it."

"We have to catch him off guard first. What I need is boys that are experts at city stalking. Good enough to keep me in sight without stepping on my heels. So they can spot anybody tagging me before he spots them."

"And strong and fast enough to take him when they do." Alfani was smiling a little. He couldn't help getting a kick out of playing one of the old games again. "I ought to be able to get you a couple professionals by this evening."

"I don't want them to know who I am," I told him. "All they have to know is what I look like and where I'll be going. Not my name or anything else about me. In case they louse up and Colin grabs one of *them*. The worst thing would be Colin finding out I was planning a double cross."

"They shouldn't know about me either, same reason. Colin's got to know I'm Arlette's father. I'll have a friend hire them. And all he tells them is to grab any guy tailing you. Because this guy might know about some jewels my friend is interested in. That'll sound close enough to possible for Colin to buy."

I nodded. Alfani hadn't gotten to where he used to be by not thinking fast. "Good enough. And these pros your friend hires—I don't want them carrying guns or knives. Colin is no good to us dead."

"Leg breakers," Alfani said. "Guys used to handling problems with just muscle. And maybe a blackjack to make sure." He looked at me thoughtfully. "Of course if your tail *is* Colin—he's always armed."

"These pros don't have to know that."

"They could get a bad surprise. Say they don't move quick enough—he'll waste them both."

"That's the chance we have to take." I couldn't get worked up about the possible termination of a couple professional leg breakers.

"You know," Alfani said reflectively, "when you got to, you can be real nasty."

I sensed more than a little respect in the way he said it. I preferred not to think what I sensed was recognition of a fellow bastard.

I was getting ready to leave when the the phone rang. It only rang once before being picked up in another room of the suite. A second later one of the bodyguards appeared in the living room doorway and told Marcel Alfani, "A guy named Fritz wants to talk to you. Won't give the rest of his name."

"Okay, I'll take it. Go hang up the other phone." Alfani started toward the one in the living room.

I said, "Let me take it."

He nodded. I picked up the phone and said, "I thought you were asleep."

"It was a nap," Fritz said dryly, "not the sleep of the dead. What are you doing there?"

"Tell you later. What's up?"

"The friend I phoned in Bangkok finally called back with a bit of information. It may be of help to Alfani, as well as in one side of our investigation."

"I'll pass it on to him. Tell me."

"Huang Yok Lin was born and raised in Thailand," Fritz said. "Before he left he was associated with an underworld gang there. According to my friend it is a particularly mysterious one, about which very little is known. The belief in some Bangkok circles is that Huang left Thailand to establish branches in Europe for that gang."

"A Chinese triad?"

"Not strictly Chinese. Mixed. With even a few Caucasian members. And not a triad, though this gang does give itself a triadlike name. It may be of use to ask around about that name, on the chance they're using the same one here in Europe."

"It's worth trying," I agreed.

"They call it the Society of the Midnight Sister."

⊠ 20 ⊠

"IN THAILAND WE ARE NINETY-FIVE PERCENT BUDDHISTS but our Buddhism digests without conflict large portions of Hinduism, tantra, animism, and any other faith, cult, or superstition that cares to contribute." Kukrit Chaudee picked a *frite* off his plate and sprinkled salt on it. "Each Thai blends these various beliefs as suits him personally. Heresy is a concept alien to our mixed culture. Any and all gifts gratefully accepted."

He popped the *frite* into his mouth, chewing and smiling.

The place we were in was on the corner of Rue Soufflot and Boul' Mich, two blocks from the Sorbonne. It had been there on my first visit to Paris at the age of four—a big, seedy, comfortable brasserie-tabac, crowded with people resting their feet and moistening their throats after strolling the Luxembourg Gardens across the street. And that it had remained—your typical, flavorful big-city sanctuary—until two years ago. Now it was a big, shiny, popular McDonald's. *Sic transit* the French way of life.

"In the Hindu pantheon," Kukrit Chaudee said, "the most feared and worshipped deity is Kali. Do you know of her?"

"A little," I said, and remembered the statue in the main room on Huang's barge. "She's a goddess of life and death."

Kukrit nodded and took a big bite out of his burger. He was a tall, merry-eyed man in his late sixties. His broad shoulders strained the seams of his scuffed leather flight jacket. He wore his battered, wide-brimmed black felt hat even inside. Probably bought in a flea market, it looked like it had belonged to some turn-of-the-century musician. Kukrit's thick gray hair curled out from under it in graceful disarray.

It was difficult to picture Kukrit Chaudee as an austere Buddhist monk with a shaved skull and an orange robe. But that was what he'd been through one period of his life. Before that he'd been a history professor at Chulalongkorn University in Bangkok. At the age of forty-seven he had decided to cleanse mind and soul by spending a year in a monastery. The year had stretched to ten, during which he'd acquired a reputation as a soothsayer, advising people on everything from love to business problems. Then he'd returned to the university.

"In broad terms," he said, "that is what Kali represents. Life and death. In detail she has as many aspects as she has arms. She is at the same time an embracing mother and the bringer of pestilence. Two of her hands offer a cup of nourishment and a flower of pure delight. Another two wield the sword of slaughter and scissors to cut off existence."

"Giver and taker," I said. "No wonder she's feared and worshipped. Sounds close to real life."

"Indeed. Benevolence and malevolence intertwined. Which accounts for the variety of names by which Kali is known. The Divine Mother and the Drinker of Blood. The Protectress and the Destroyer. The Gift-Bestowing Tree and the Dark Goddess of Fear."

Kukrit salted another *frite* and ate it delicately. "Some also call her the Midnight Sister—dividing night and day, yesterday from tomorrow, belonging to neither yet both."

It was dark outside. Kukrit had been working late in the library of the Sorbonne, where he was taking a sabbatical year researching the background of French involvement in Southeast Asia. I had picked him up there and he was the one who'd suggested McDonald's for our talk. Kukrit considered its food wondrously exotic. I had to say one thing—it was the cheapest dinner I ever bought for an informant.

"Midnight Sister," he repeated. "That is the derivation of the name used by the organization you are interested in. Underworld syndicates in my part of the world like to give themselves such picturesque names. There are many in Thailand. Most with their origins elsewhere. Hong Kong, Singapore, Taiwan. This one is homegrown. Its membership is as mixed as our population and culture but its leadership is Thailand-born Chinese."

"How do you know about it?" I asked.

"At one time the Society of the Midnight Sister was at war with a Bangkok triad. Over counterfeiting antique European furniture for export. Using Malayan mahogany and Thai teak and some expert wood craftsmen in Bangkok. There were only a few of those craftsmen good enough. The conflict was over which organization would control their services. A leader of the Society of the Midnight Sister came to consult me."

"About how to conduct the war."

"Yes, but I would never give advice to help a criminal endeavor. I only told him that his organization would lose to the triad. Which it did."

"What was the name of this man?"

Kukrit told me. The name didn't mean anything to me. I asked if he had ever heard of Huang Yok Lin. He hadn't.

"I only knew this one man," Kukrit told me. "After my prediction about the outcome of his war with the triad proved accurate, he continued to consult me. About personal matters and his legitimate businesses. But in the course of that I did learn more about the Society of the Midnight Sister. It recovered from its defeat and continued to prosper with its other rackets. Gambling, extortion, and prostitution. Heroin and loan-sharking."

"And smuggling people to Europe," I added.

"Yes, that too."

"It's this syndicate's operations here in Europe that interest me," I told Kukrit.

But that proved disappointing. He knew only of the organization's rackets in Thailand. Other than that and the meaning of its name he couldn't add anything to what I'd learned since giving Marcel Alfani the name yesterday.

Which didn't add up to much either. So far Huang's gang seemed to be working only with and against other Orientals, avoiding contact and conflict with Alfani's European mobsters. They knew of three places where the Midnight Sister Society was operating: Paris, Antwerp, and Hamburg. There were rumors it used the ports of the latter two for bringing in illegal aliens and heroin and other smuggled goods. The Alfani connection hadn't come through with anything else and wasn't likely to, and Kukrit Chaudee didn't have any further information of even peripheral value.

Just so the fortune I'd spent on his burger and french fries wouldn't be a total loss I asked before we parted how he'd made his predictions back in his monk-soothsayer days.

"With running water and floating leaves, palmistry and astrology, the phases of the moon and the stone of heaven." Kukrit grinned and winked at me. "In reality all those were simply to give the questioners confidence. In truth the answers just came to me, without thought and almost immediately. And usually proved correct; I don't know why."

"I'm looking for a young woman named Christine Boyer," I told him. "Where is she?"

"With the goats," Kukrit answered promptly.

"What does that mean?"

"I don't know," he said lightly. "That's all I get."

He went down into the Métro and I walked back to where I'd left my car. I didn't check the immediate vicinity around or behind me to see if anyone was shadowing me again. The two leg breakers one of Alfani's mob friends had come up with were supposed to be somewhere around taking care of that.

My car was parked in Place de l'Estrapade. The little *place* was deserted and dim at that time of night. Some trees had been strategically planted to block off the streetlamps. I was halfway across it, reaching into my pocket for the car keys, when my shadow materialized.

Not Colin. A pair of young Thai boxers.

They moved fast and silently, closing in on me from both sides.

🔳 21 🔳

APPARENTLY THEY'D BEEN ORDERED TO STOP SHADOWING and grab me—without damaging me more than necessary in the process. They didn't have weapons and they didn't use their feet on me. They came at me with their hands open to seize my arms. Their hands missed because by the time they finished reaching I was flat on my back in the middle of the street, snatching a pistol out of my belt holster. The speed of my reaction paid testimony to all those months of heart-in-mouth Nam patrols, where you learned to go to ground at the first hint of a scary sound or movement.

The gun I aimed up at them was the one from my apartment. A compact Beretta with its magazine fully packed. Fourteen 9mm cartridges. I didn't want to fire any of them because it was happening too fast with no time for careful aim and the shots might kill. I was more eager to question them. But they didn't know that. When I yelled "Freeze!" they hesitated.

It wasn't much of a hesitation—but long enough for the two leg breakers to loom behind them. About time. They were head and shoulders taller than the Thai pair. One swung a blackjack. The Thai he swung it at sidestepped. But not far enough. The blackjack whacked into a shoulder. The sound of it crunching bone was painful to hear. The Thai boxer stumbled a few steps with one arm dangling helplessly and went down on his knees.

The other leg breaker had clamped a lock on the second Thai's neck with his long, thick arms. Mistake. The Thai's elbow jerked back. The leg breaker let go of him and sat down hard in the street, then lay down on his side with both forearms pressed against his middle while he gasped for air.

The thug with the blackjack jumped for the Thai who'd done that. But he didn't reach him. The other Thai came up off his knees, arm still dangling, and kicked. His heel connected with the side of the blackjacker's head. The head snapped back further than any neck was engineered to let a head move. The guy the head had belonged to toppled over and didn't move again.

The Thai with the ruined shoulder jumped over him and ran into one of the narrow side streets leading away from the *place*. I was trying to take aim at his legs when the remaining Thai kicked the Beretta out of my hand. Just like that. One second he was standing on both feet turned away from me and the next my right hand was numb and empty and the gun was in flight. It bounced off the front tire of my car as the next kick came at my head.

I dodged it and caught the kicker's ankle left-handed, gave it a twist and a shove. He went spinning away, both feet off the ground, and executed a fast roll immediately after landing on his back. He was coming back up on his feet when I scrambled to the fallen Beretta. The fingers of my right hand were still too numbed to handle it. I switched the pistol to my left hand. By then the one with the wrecked shoulder had vanished and the other was sprinting away in the opposite direction.

I wasn't good enough left-handed to be certain of hitting his legs in that bad light with him moving that fast. But he wasn't aware of that handicap. He twisted into an alley to escape the shots he expected. That was fine. I knew where that alley went and he obviously didn't. It dead-ended at a storage shed attached to the rear of a tool and garden supplies outlet. The place would be locked up tight at that hour.

I launched to my feet and raced after him. When I turned into the alley, he was down at the other end, frantically looking around for a way out and not finding any. He heard me coming through toward him, spun away from me, and drove a hip-high kick at the shed's locked door.

I've kicked my way through a few doors in my time. But this one was solid metal and so was its frame. It would have broken my foot before it gave. His kick ripped out the hinges. He jumped through the opening and was swallowed up by the darkness in the shed.

I dived in seconds later, landing stretched out on the floor inside. Doing a fast roll as something swooshed over my head. It struck the wall next to me with a force that tore it out of his hand and fell across my chest. It was a hoe handle. My right hand was functional enough by then to grip one end of it. With the Beretta ready in my left hand I rose to my feet.

His shadowy figure came through the darkness at me. I drove the hoe handle at him like a spear. It was ripped away from me by a kick that just missed my chest. I jumped sideways and bumped against a heavy bench.

"I still have the gun," I said, tight and fast. "I'll shoot you dead if you make me."

The shadowy figure moved away abruptly. An instant later I couldn't see or hear him. But I knew what he would be doing. Searching for another way out. He wouldn't find it because there wasn't any. Only the door he'd broken through to get into the dark shed. He couldn't use that without being outlined in it long enough to be an easy target for my gun. There was no way for him to get out again without eliminating me first.

I needed to find a light switch before he realized that. I started moving backward around the heavy bench, feeling behind me with my right hand. Something stabbed into my palm. I winced and stopped a gasp. Then I reached out more carefully, investigating what I'd jabbed my hand on. It was a big roll of barbed wire resting loosely on the bench.

Silently resuming my move around the bench, I stopped when I had it between me and the bulk of the room. I scraped my shoe on the rough wooden flooring and waited. Then I did it again.

He was too close for comfort when I finally made out his figure coming at me, very fast. I tipped over the bench, spilling the barbed wire on the floor between us. There was a surprised yell, and then the thud when he tripped over it and hit the floor—followed by a scream.

I backed up against the wall, felt along it until I found the light switch and flicked it on. He was thrashing around on the floor, tangled in barbed wire, bleeding from a dozen small punctures.

When I walked over to him, he began a steady, savage flow of curses.

"That's a relief," I said. "I was worried you might not speak French but you're fluent. That makes everything easier."

I used the Beretta to knock him out before beginning the job of extricating him from the wire.

⊠ 22 ⊠

His name was Phoon Jamsai. Lying there on the studio couch in Max Novak's study, he didn't look like the deadly weapon he was. He appeared a sleepily friendly, harmless youth. Utterly relaxed on the couch, he gazed at the ceiling with a dreamy smile, as though watching a mildly entertaining film up there. His voice was lazily contented. His pupils had shrunk to tiny dots.

I had brought him there handcuffed and blindfolded. We had kept him that way while Max Novak did the preliminary work on him. Novak was a research chemist specializing in mind-control drugs. He was employed by France's biggest pharmaceutical company, in a subdivision with an ongoing project for the DST, the government's internal intelligence agency. His debt to Fritz Donhoff went back ten years, to a situation in which Fritz had removed the threat of a blackmailer trying to pry company secrets out of him.

Novak had used the vein in Phoon's left wrist for injecting the first hypodermic load of drugs. When that had rendered Phoon quiescent, I'd removed the handcuffs and Novak had tended to the puncture wounds from the barbed wire. The second injection was into the muscles high on Phoon's right shoulder. After that Novak retired to his living room and I closed the study door and took off Phoon's blindfold.

I remained standing by the head of the couch while Fritz,

seated in an armchair beside Phoon, conducted most of the interrogation. The drugs achieved optimum results when the questioner was a fatherly authority figure. Fritz's age in conjunction with his heavy rumbling voice—which could change from warmly approving to hurt-disappointed when answers were slow in coming—made him perfect for this.

The easy questions first, allowing Phoon to talk about himself. He was from a hill tribe in the impoverished northeast area of Thailand. His farmer father had sold him to child buyers in Chiang Mai when he was ten. Even then he had been unusually strong and agile. The men who'd purchased Phoon decided to have him trained in the arts of Thai boxing. By fourteen his prowess at it had attracted the interest of members of the Society of the Midnight Sister. They had paid off his debt to his owners and inducted him into the Society after he had used his skills to kill his first man for them.

After that the Society had moved him down to Bangkok, where he had become an enforcer for its loan-shark and protection rackets. Until six years ago, when the investigations of a DEA agent stationed in Thailand had become an annoyance to the Society. Phoon had eliminated the annoyance, killing the agent in what was made to look like a barroom brawl. But a witness to the fight recognized Phoon and gave the police his identity.

The Society had quickly gotten Phoon out of Thailand, flying him to Paris with false papers. Waiting for him in Paris was Huang Yok Lin.

Under Fritz's patient, paternal questioning, Phoon revealed that Huang was in charge of the Society's operations in Europe, dividing his time between Paris, Antwerp, and Hamburg. In each of the three cities Huang had several lieutenants handling different aspects of the Society's affairs. Each aspect was tightly compartmentalized. That way if a member got in trouble, he couldn't tell the police about any operations except the few he'd been directly involved in himself. Not that he'd be likely to anyway. The Society's vengeance would be terrible—reaching not only the squealer but his family, in Europe and back in Thailand.

Huang had assigned Phoon to one of his Paris lieutenants. Phoon had remained in France since then, continuing to work as an enforcer but also occasionally taking part in robberies.

"Was one of those the big jewel robbery in Antibes?" Fritz asked him.

"Oh, yes," Phoon said. He seemed to be especially happy whenever he could give Fritz an affirmative answer to any question. "With four other members of our Midnight Sister Society—and Dédé Colin." Phoon almost frowned when he pronounced that name. "A bad man . . . untrustworthy . . ."

"Colin is very bad," Fritz agreed. "Did you know him well?"

"No . . . I met him only two days . . . no, three days . . . before Antibes." Phoon's knowledge of Colin's doings before and after the Antibes robbery, Fritz's soothing questions revealed, was limited to hearsay.

One thing he'd heard explained why the European police hadn't been able to turn up any word on Colin after his killing of the informer Gaetan Mora. He had spent that year in Bangkok, waiting out the hottest period of the hunt for him. While there Colin had done some jobs for the Midnight Sister Society. Eliminating triad competitors. In situations where the Society didn't want to be identified as the source of the killings.

"Why did he come back to Europe?" Fritz asked.

"I . . . don't know." Phoon didn't like saying that to Fritz.

"That is very disappointing," Fritz chided sadly.

"I'm sorry. . . ." Phoon sounded ready to cry.

Fritz patted his arm. "That's all right, Phoon. Perhaps Colin became homesick. Go on to what you do know."

"I know the Society arranged for his return," Phoon offered eagerly. "To Antwerp first. Huang already had the Antibes robbery planned. But the five of us selected for it were arguing. Over which should be the leader. Huang brought Colin down from Antwerp and made him our leader. An outsider . . . to stop the jealousy between us."

"Was that when Colin met Christine Boyer—before Huang brought him down from Antwerp?"

Phoon looked troubled and didn't speak.

"You must tell me," Fritz said sternly. "You know I need your help."

Phoon's silence, it developed, was a reluctance to tell Fritz he didn't know. "I have never been to Antwerp," he said finally, almost stammering. "I never met her. Nobody told me about her and Colin."

"That is a good answer," Fritz reassured him.

Phoon looked relieved. He answered questions about the jewel robbery quickly. Most of it we knew. Up to when the gang had left the Antibes villa with their loot. "I left with two of our men in one car," he said. "The other two went with Colin and the jewels in a second car. Nobody ever saw those two again. Not even their corpses. Maybe Colin buried them together with the jewels. . . . A bad man," he repeated, his tone prim. "Huang was very upset about him."

"I assume," Fritz said soothingly, "that Huang organized Colin's escape from prison. Am I right?"

"Oh, yes . . . It was so Huang could seize him and make him tell where the jewels are."

"How can that be?" Fritz sounded puzzled, a bit unbelieving. "I know Huang *didn't* seize Colin."

"Because Colin didn't climb *inside* the helicopter! He hung on to the outside all the way from the prison. . . . Until it was coming in low to land where Huang and the others were waiting. Colin jumped off just before the helicopter reached them and ran into the woods. They chased him but couldn't find him."

I tried a question of my own: "Who gave Colin that gun inside the prison?"

Phoon regarded me vaguely, as though he didn't know who I was. He didn't reply.

Fritz repeated my question. Phoon turned his head to look at Fritz. "I had no part in Huang's arrangements for the prison escape. No one except those involved were told anything about it."

"You are being very helpful to me now," Fritz told him with tender approval.

Phoon beamed. "Thank you."

But after that Fritz's questioning began to bump up against more things Phoon didn't know than things he did. He and his partner—whose name was Prasert—had been one of a number of teams searching for Colin. He didn't know how the other teams were going about it. Phoon and Prasert had been assigned to shadow me, in the hope they would spot me making contact with Colin. If that happened, they were to grab Colin.

"That was a dangerous assignment," Fritz said. "Why didn't you carry weapons to help you do it?"

"Huang forbade it. Prasert is as skilled at martial arts as I am. We were told to use those skills in taking Colin. Huang wants to be sure he's not killed by accident before he tells where the jewels are."

Their orders had been changed after a couple days of shadowing me without a sign of Colin. I was to be grabbed instead, for questioning about Colin's whereabouts. I didn't let myself dwell on how the interrogation would have turned out, with me not having any answers for them.

The place they were to have taken me to was one of the private rooms over Cozy's, one of the hot Paris discotheques for well-heeled night crawlers. It was owned by a man named Julien Boisson, who had lived in Bangkok for some years before returning home to Paris and opening his joint. He paid a percentage of his take to one of the Paris mobs to be allowed to run it. But not even the underworld was aware that Boisson had become part of the Midnight Sister Society while in Thailand. Nor that the floor above the disco was a safe house for some of the Society's gunmen.

Phoon couldn't tell us whether Huang was in Paris now. Or where he stayed when he was. Boisson was the one who would have contacted Huang if I or Colin were brought in.

The most vital things Phoon didn't know concerned Christine Boyer. He'd heard that Huang had people hunting for her but he didn't have any idea why he wanted her found. He didn't know how or where the search for her was being carried out, except that Boisson had some part in directing it for Huang.

I blindfolded Phoon Jamsai again before taking him away from Novak's place. I didn't bother putting the handcuffs back on him. The drugs pumped into his system were still too active for that to be necessary. He was utterly cooperative under their influence. He was also too uncoordinated to walk two steps by himself. I had to more than half carry him out to my car.

And carry him out of it when I stopped the car a dozen blocks away. I settled Phoon down in a service alley between a couple large garbage bins. He appeared to find that even more comfortable than the couch in Novak's study. He was asleep before I walked back to the car.

I pulled over to the next phone booth I came to and called Fritz's number. Arlette had a message waiting for me. From Lee To Hyun, the conscience-stricken sweatshop operator. Lee wanted me to phone him as soon as possible.

◙ 23 ◙

He had left two phone numbers. The first was at his sweatshop. Lee had left for the night. I tried his home number next. He picked up in the middle of the second ring.

"It is about that man we discussed," he told me after I identified myself.

"The one who lost his garment business and has to push clothes racks these days."

"Yes—I didn't find him at his place last night. But I chanced to run into him in the garment district late this afternoon. I told him about your anxiety to find Christine. He says he knows things about her that should help you."

"Does that mean he's ready to tell me about them?"

"Well . . ." Lee hesitated. "He feels that if it is important to you, you should pay him generously for the information. Please do not think badly of him for that attitude. A man struck down by financial adversity can become desperate for any source of money."

"I can't give him enough to put him back in business," I said. "If his information's good, I'll pay what I can without borrowing from the Rockefellers."

"What you pay him is between the two of you. None of my business. My concern in this matter ends here—with performing a favor. I hope for Christine as well as you."

128

"You have my number and my partner's," I told him. "If you ever need a favor in return, feel free to call on us."

"As a matter of fact," Lee said, "two truckloads of my goods have been hijacked in the last six weeks. If you could—"

"We can discuss that later," I interrupted him. "After this case is completed. I'll contact you again when it is. You still haven't given me this garment man's name or address."

"Etienne Soulier," Lee told me, and gave me his house address. "It is a small apartment Etienne moved to after his bankruptcy. He should be there now. He told me he would make himself dinner there tonight and wait for you."

The address was near the Sentier Métro station on the edge of the garment district. The narrow street ran downhill from the Rue Réaumur. Both sides were lined with food shops. A good deal of the space in the old buildings above them was taken by one- and two-room fringe businesses that serviced the rag trade. By day it was a lively street. At night it was as shut down as an abandoned mine shaft.

The building where Etienne Soulier lived had a cobbled entry wide enough to accommodate the horse-drawn freight wagons that once used it. Small signs were nailed to the walls flanking the entry, with the names of interior shops and directions for finding them. Melanie & Mireille—Stylish Buttons, fourth floor left, second court. Walkyrie Ribbons, front court second floor. Dora Benzara—Parfumerie de Luxe, third floor rear court.

Also Anna Yershov—Voyante Diplomée, first court, stairway B. I wondered if having a diploma made Anna Yershov more farseeing than dropout clairvoyants. Maybe she could tell me what Kurkrit Chaudee meant about Christine Boyer being with the goats.

There was no sign for Etienne Soulier but Lee had given me detailed instructions. One dim court led into another, and then another, penetrating the heart of the block, walled by the backs of high connected buildings with cracked, weather-stained walls. The first two courts contained one-car garages and multiple staircases leading up in different directions. The last court was a dead end with three staircases, a shoe repair shop, and two extralarge garages that had been burnt out a long time ago. The fire-blackened, heat-twisted truck inside one of them looked vintage 1930.

I found a timer light button inside stairway A. It flicked on a tiny bulb at the top. I climbed worn stone steps. The same bulb made it just possible to find my way along a corridor with no carpet or even linoleum covering its splintering wooden floor. I was finally beginning to feel sorry for the bankrupt Monsieur Soulier.

His card was tacked to the door of his apartment. A business card with only his name readable. The name of his defunct company and its phone number had been scratched out with a red ballpoint pen. I knocked—and got no response. He had told Lee he would stay home and wait for me tonight. I tried knocking one more time. Nothing.

I began to feel sorrier about Etienne Soulier. Of course he could have run out of cigarettes and gone out to the tabac still open near the Métro for another pack. Or he had a dog and was taking him on his last necessity walk of the day. I didn't think so. What I thought was I'd gotten there too late.

I drew my pistol and held it down by my thigh before testing the doorknob with my left hand. Sure enough, the door was unlocked. I waited until the tiny light bulb down the hall flicked out. Then I took a deep breath, shoved open the door, and dodged inside. So far so good. Nothing moved in the darkness around me. No sound except the thud of my heart against my eardrums. I felt the wall and found a light switch, dodged aside again as I snapped it on.

The room was empty. Of life and almost of furniture. There was a kitchen table and a single straight-back chair and a bookcase. The bookcase overflowed with paperbacks.

The poor man's recreation. Soulier hadn't even been able to save a TV set from his financial wreckage.

Dinner was on the table. A soup dish heaped with spaghetti in tomato sauce. An opened bottle of wine, half full. A wineglass, entirely filled. I touched a finger to the spaghetti. Stone cold.

I moved through the rest of his apartment. It wasn't a long walk. A closet-size kitchen. A bedroom with an iron-frame bed, large bureau, freestanding closet, no chair. It was separated from the bathroom facilities by a curtain. Etienne Soulier's clothes and shoes were scattered across the floor between the bedroom and the bathroom area. Some blood, too. Not much. Soulier was in the bathtub.

One naked arm hung over the side of the tub, the hand touching the floor. Both naked feet stuck out over the end of the tub. I looked once at what had been done to his fingers and some toes and didn't look at those again.

The tub was two-thirds full of water. Soulier's face was below the surface. His mouth was wide open and so were his eyes. I wondered what price he had thought his information might be worth. It wouldn't have occurred to him that he would be the one paying for it. With his pain and his life.

I didn't think it was Colin who'd done this. He liked to kill and he liked terrifying people with the threat of killing. He wasn't a torturer. He hadn't laid a finger on Marie Vernon while prying information out of her on that barge. His chilling smile and reputation did all the persuading he needed. That was his crooked pride.

It had to be Huang's people who had worked on Etienne Soulier.

Whatever he had known about Christine Boyer, they had it now. No question about that. They wouldn't have let him die before he told them all he had to tell. I didn't know how much or little that had been. But I did know his information put them that much closer to her than I was. They were going to get her, unless I got very lucky, very soon.

I went through the apartment with some thoroughness but more speed. My nerves were rubbed too raw for sticking around there longer than absolutely essential. As I'd expected, it was wasted effort. There was nothing of any use to me.

I did find Etienne Soulier's wallet. It was on the floor beside his jacket. I used my handkerchief in picking it up. If there'd been cash in it, they'd taken it. All that was left were his identification papers.

I wrapped my handkerchief around the wallet and put it in a side pocket of my jacket before leaving.

What I had in mind wouldn't do Soulier any good. He was beyond caring about a little retaliation. But I wasn't.

⊠ 24 ⊠

INDOLENCE HAS ITS USES. MORE TIME SHOULD BE ALLO-cated to it. It relaxes the muscles and calms the nerves and clears the harassed brain. It gives you a breather between things that oppress and depress. Like a girl who'd taken more than her share of dirty punches from life and was due for more unless I found a way to get to her first. Like a successful businessman reduced to penury and then tortured and drowned in his own bathtub.

Sleeping, swimming, reading while sipping a light drink, all are fine aids to constructive indolence. My favorite is floating on the sea while my mind floats in nothing at all, just watching the clouds change shape.

Lacking clouds and sea I had to make do with sitting inside the terrace of a Champs-Élysées brasserie, sipping at my second Scotch on the rocks and watching the crowds go by. Well-dressed people on their way to bars and nightclubs or on their way home after the last night movies let out. I don't frequent that area much except on business. I'm a Left Bank man and the Champs-Élysées is Right Bank. So the odds were against my being jarred out of my indolence there by genial passersby recognizing me. That was a help. I felt too grouchy for idle chitchat.

Which meant I wasn't doing too good a job of letting it all go. Nagging thoughts intruded in spite of my best efforts to achieve nirvana. Like what the police might be doing with the corpse in the tub. I'd left Etienne Soulier's door wide open when I went out, and I'd made the anonymous call to the cops after putting some distance between his body and myself. They should be there by now. . . .

I reminded myself sternly of Ray Knight of the Mets and his words of wisdom: Concentration is the ability to think about absolutely nothing when it's absolutely necessary.

It was necessary. But not easy.

Etienne Soulier's wallet was still in my pocket. That could wait a little longer. It would have to. I had phoned Fritz's number after calling the law. Fritz had answered and told me Arlette wasn't around. According to the note she'd left on his desk she'd gone out twenty minutes before he returned from Max Novak's place.

Her note said something important had come up and she'd gone to check it out. And that if I called or showed, she would like me to meet her at this brasserie on the Champs-Élysées.

I had been waiting there for an hour and Arlette still hadn't arrived. The lights on the Arc de Triomphe had gone off. It was after midnight and she was God knew where doing God knew what in a dark and dangerous city infested with torturers and killers who'd like to get their hands on her.

I told myself Arlette had a couple bodyguards with her, courtesy of one of Marcel Alfani's old pals. I told myself these two couldn't possibly be as unequal to the task as the pair of leg breakers who'd gotten clobbered when they'd tried to take the Thai boxers off me. I told myself that at least the pair with Arlette were armed.

Conjecture was futile because I didn't know where she was. Therefore, indolence. A lumpishness of mind and body. Restorative. If it could be achieved.

I tried to take another sip of my Scotch and found the glass was empty. I had drunk it all without noticing. Bad sign.

One of Arlette's bodyguards appeared in the entrance of

the brasserie. The young one named Arnie, with the big shoulders and the knife scar that cut diagonally across his lips and chin. His hands were out of sight in the deep pockets of his topcoat. He looked around and finally spotted me. I nodded that I'd already checked out the place and it seemed all right. Arnie looked back over his shoulder and said something.

Arlette came in and my mood lifted. Even more than it always did when she was around. Arlette Alfani, nature's best formula for restorative relaxation.

She was followed closely by her other watchdog. The older and smaller one named Felix, with the graying hair and sleepy eyes. Felix only had one hand in the depths of a topcoat pocket. A one-gun hood. Confidence born of experience.

I hugged and kissed Arlette. Maybe I put too much into it for the middle of a crowded brasserie. She pulled back a little and eyed me curiously. "Something wrong, Pierre-Ange?"

"Just past my bedtime," I said, the guy in the tub momentarily forgotten. I signaled a passing waiter as I sat down with Arlette. She ordered a *ballon* of red. I smiled at her and decided I didn't need another Scotch.

There was a man occupying the small table next to us. Felix spoke softly to him. The man looked at his sleepy eyes and at Arnie's scarred face. Then he stood up and headed for the bar, carrying his drink with him. Felix and Arnie sat down at the table and watched the door and windows.

"I'm sorry I'm late getting here," Arlette said as she opened her shoulder bag. "This took longer than I expected."

She got an envelope out of her bag. "Pauline Jacobs phoned from Brussels Airport while you and Fritz were out. She'd just given this to a stewardess on a Sabena flight to Paris. I went to Orly to pick it up. Since then I've been checking it out."

From the envelope Arlette extracted a color picture cut out

of a magazine. She put it down in front of me. "The girl in the picture," she said, "is Christine Boyer."

She couldn't have been more than seventeen or eighteen when the picture was taken. She stood close beside a man in his late twenties and was smiling a bit shyly into the camera. Very pretty, small, and slender, her head barely as high as the man's shoulder. She wore a black and white sailor blouse with a white miniskirt and black tights. Auburn curls dangled around her delicate elfin face. If this was Christine Boyer, I understood why Colin had found it difficult to believe she was half-Oriental. Nothing in her features hinted at it.

The man in the picture with her had a rugged, wide-boned face framed by a tousled Prince Valiant haircut. He was wearing an open tweed jacket over a maroon crewneck sweater and dark blue slacks. One of his arms was draped around Christine Boyer's shoulders. There was a martini glass in his other hand. It looked empty and he looked like he'd emptied enough others before that to be pleasantly half-sloshed.

The picture had no caption and there was nothing in its background to suggest where it had been taken.

"Where did Pauline get this?" I asked Arlette.

"From the landlord of the place where Christine lived in Antwerp. The apartment rented for her by Alfred Streuvels, Huang's gambler-partner. The landlord owns that building and several others on the same block. Pauline didn't talk to him before because he was taking a holiday in Greece. He got back today and she went to see him. He told her Christine disappeared at the same time Streuvels was found dead. And she didn't take any of her things from the apartment with her."

"Colin probably moved her out too fast to give her time for that," I said. "He could always buy her whatever she needed down here in Paris." I pointed to the magazine clipping. "This was among the things she left behind?"

Arlette nodded. "The landlord boxed all her stuff and put it in the basement. In case Christine ever came back for it, but she never did. He let Pauline go through all of it and she found this. The landlord says it was in a drawer under her blouses. He says the girl in the picture is definitely Christine Boyer."

I turned the clipping over. On the other side was part of an article in French about the renovation of a classic château near Fontainebleau. I felt the quality of the magazine paper between thumb and fingers. "Could be *Paris-Match* or *Jours de France*."

"I figured those were the logical magazines to start with," Arlette said. "And that since they're such big rivals either would have complete files of the other. I phoned a woman I used to go to school with. She's now assistant to the art director of *Jours de France* near here. We met there and she went through back copies of her magazine while I did the same with *Paris-Match*. Working backward from the date Christine Boyer left Antwerp. That clipping is from an issue of *Paris-Match* three years ago."

"Nice work."

"Less public flattery and more private affection, if you please."

"Glutton."

"Yes." Arlette reached into her shoulder bag again and brought out a folded copy of *Paris-Match*. "I stole it from *Jours de France*, so treat it gently. I want to put it back later." She unfolded the magazine and opened it to the right page and handed it to me.

The article was a four-page photo coverage of a New Year's party at the Parisian town house of Nicole de Scouarnac. Queen bee of an illustrious family and its fortune. Equally well known as a patron of the arts, young widow of a former prime minister, and arbiter of French social status. Who was in and who was out, in the upper strata of the capital, could hinge on whether you received an invitation to one of her exclusive gatherings.

But, the short editorial introduction pointed out, she was no snob. She liked to mix high society's A-list with stars of stage and screen and government. And even an occasional up-and-coming painter or sculptor. Her mansion in town and her château out by Milly-la-Forêt were filled with works by now-famous contemporary artists that her generosity had helped along the bumpy road from obscurity to fashionable acclaim.

A large photograph of Nicole de Scouarnac on the magnificent entrance staircase of her town house graced the first page of the article. She was in her late forties, a handsome woman with a turn-off smile. She looked too sophisticated to take a deep breath. Crushed with boredom since age ten. By which age she'd been gifted with so many of life's goodies with so little effort that the delight and sadness centers of her brain had been totally zapped.

The caption under the picture said the diamond-and-sapphire necklace she was wearing was insured for half a million francs and her one-of-a-kind gown, created by one of the world's top couturiers for this occasion only, was rumored to have cost the equivalent of twenty thousand dollars.

The next two pages consisted of people enjoying the festivities, with captions of their big-bore names for readers unable to identify all the heavyweights of high society. The final page was a collage of lesser guests, none with individual captions—merely a collective caption for the entire assortment: "More of the Beautiful People sharing the New Year with Nicole de Scouarnac."

The picture of Christine Boyer and the slightly sloshed young man with his arm around her was part of the collage. I noted that he seemed to be the only male guest not wearing a formal dinner jacket and tie, and she was the only woman pictured without a fabulous evening gown.

"I have a friend," Arlette told me, "who knows Nicole de Scouarnac. Sandrine de Cabrel—she's a countess, but she doesn't lean on it too much. I can probably get you an introduction from her."

"Arriving as someone socially acceptable would be helpful," I admitted. "Get me in by the front door instead of having to go all the way around to the servants' entrance. Call your friend."

"I already did. Sandrine's butler says she's away, but she'll be back tomorrow morning."

"Tomorrow morning will be soon enough. Maybe I should also mention to this Scouarnac woman that I'm a friend of yours. After all, you were once a countess, too, by brief marriage."

"It wouldn't help. My ex-husband is too minor a count, and Sicilian—far below that crowd's concept of social acceptability."

I gave the magazine back to Arlette and asked her to take it to my apartment for me.

A small worry line deepened between her eyebrows, and just as quickly disappeared. "You're not coming with us," she said with deliberate lack of expression.

"I've got one more thing to take care of," I said, and looked to Felix and Arnie as I stood up. They were on their feet a split second later, without appearing hurried. "Stay awake," I told them. "The vermin we're dealing with are getting rougher."

Felix just nodded, once. Arnie strolled over to the entrance door and waited there, looking out at the street. Both hands were back in his pockets.

Arlette put the magazine in her bag, got up, and kissed my cheek lightly. "Be careful."

25

COZY'S WAS JUST OFF RUE DE LAPPE, NEAR PLACE DE LA
Bastille. The area immediately surrounding the Bastille used
to be considered seedy. But lately the media spokespersons
in charge of keeping the public informed about what's trendy
had taken to calling the neighborhood scruffy-chic. The
change anticipates a rush of culture and customers to the
Bastille quarter when the second opera of Paris finishes being
built there.

So far the cultural level hasn't risen noticeably but the
prices have. Groceries and shoe-repair shops have become
boutiques and art galleries. Bistros have shined themselves
up. Restaurants, nightclubs, and jazz joints proliferate. Tourists from as far away as Baltimore or St.-Germain-des-Pres
infiltrate.

I didn't head straight to Cozy's disco. First I dropped into
a bar two blocks the other side of Place de la Bastille. It was
called The Old Soldier and it was still pigheadedly resisting
the gentrification going on around it. The owner, Edouard
Oger, had been in the Resistance with Fritz but he wasn't the
old soldier of the bar's name. Oger claimed the place was
started by one of Bonaparte's grenadiers back in 1813. The
bar looked old enough, so he may not have been lying.

Oger was a retired police detective and a good portion of
his regulars were off-duty cops. There were two inspectors

from the Brigade Criminelle at the bar when I came in. They were unwinding from a tough tour of night duty. It was almost two hours since they'd gotten off, but they still hadn't unwound enough to go home and crawl in bed with their wives.

Oger introduced me to them as a former cop and a good pal. Their names were Gauberti and Miol. I told them I had a yen to gawk at the raunchy revels of the disco freaks but felt funny about going there alone. I said I was flush at the moment and ready to spring for a bottle of champagne in exchange for genial company. Were they interested? They were.

Gauberti, Miol, and I walked it from The Old Soldier. Around the Bastille and into Rue de Lappe with its horde of night wanderers. Past a Spanish restaurant with flamenco dancers, a jazz joint with a small band good enough for Chicago at its jazziest, a British pub spewing the odor of fish-and-chips into the cold night air.

There was the usual crowd in front of Cozy's. The rejected ones. The disco's big doorkeeper wore a short mink coat and had a sharp eye and high standards. You had to be a celebrity, or an entertaining-looking freak, or extremely pretty of any sex, or stylishly scandalous, or a wealthy "fun person" with a party of spenders to get in.

We didn't strike the doorkeeper as belonging to any of those categories. He made a push-away gesture with both big hands and shook his head at us. The crowd outside grinned happily. Rejection loves company. Gauberti got out his wallet and flipped it open to show his credentials.

The doorkeeper's expression changed to a weak smile. "Is there any problem, officers?"

"Not unless you try to keep us out," Miol told him with the bored voice and impatient stare cops get with the badge.

The doorkeeper opened the door a few inches and spoke quickly to someone inside. Then he opened all the way and gestured us in. We were met inside by a small man wearing a dark green leisure suit, an orange bow tie, and a worried face. "I'm Maurice, the manager," he said. "How can I help you officers?" His French had a cockney accent.

"We want a table where we can see what's going on," I told him. An innocent enough request. But coming from what he assumed was a cop, he could read uncomfortable meanings into it.

"If there has been some complaint," he said nervously, "I'm sure we can . . ."

"A table," I repeated. My cop voice and stare were still as intimidating as Miol's. "And a good bottle of champagne. At a reasonable price. I'll pay for that. But the table's on the house. Respect for the law."

Maurice swallowed, nodded, and led us through red-plush curtains, past old bathtubs filled with dirt sprouting big tropical plants under an assortment of antique chandeliers. The curved booth he took us to had a view of the dance floor. We just managed to squeeze into it. Gauberti's and Miol's shoulders were as big as mine. Maurice went off for the champagne, still worried.

The joint was jumping. The noise level pounded the brain. People yelled to be heard by people next to them over the music. Dicso-funk revved up to decibel overkill. The senses drowned in it and the psychedelic lighting effects flashing from red, black, and purple ceiling spots.

"You were right," Gauberti shouted in my ear as we took in the action, "a real freak show."

The dancers were into show-off costumes and private ecstasies, the insistent beat from the big amplifiers numbing their minds and raping their bodies, detached as they were from their partners but wired into their audience. Orgiastic excess as an art form. A trio of transvestites in multicolored spangled leotards were doing slow-motion acrobatics. A girl in a big mustard-yellow wig had pulled the front of her blouse down so her breasts could bob free with every prancing step. A muscular guy wearing a leather jockstrap and some interesting tattoos was twirling a woman around to make the skirt of her black-sequin gown flare up and show she wasn't wearing panties. Cozy's had a reputation for getting raunchier as the night got older.

"Look at that one." Miol pointed out a voluptuous blonde who was managing to gyrate amazingly despite the tightness of her see-through black lace dress. "She's not wearing *anything* underneath."

"Sure she is," Gauberti said. "That patch of black velvet covering her kitten."

"That's not velvet, that's *her*." Miol and Gauberti continued to watch her dance, trying to decide who was right.

Few of the celebrities present that night were among the performers on the dance floor. Most were at their tables, drinking and fondling one another while they watched the show. None of them were what Nicole de Scouarnac would have considered A-list people. But their faces were instantly familiar to the public.

Like the TV actress necking with the pretty ballerina who was said to be the reason for her recent, much-publicized divorce.

Like the popular singer, now in his late sixties, seated with his twenty-four-year-old sixth wife and two girls of about eighteen. One of the girls was perched on his knees and the other had her head on his shoulder and his hand in both of hers on her lap. His wife stared at her drink, gloomy with the knowledge that she was getting too old to compete.

Maurice returned carrying three champagne glasses, followed by a waitress in striped pajamas carrying our bottle in an ice bucket. They set their burdens down on our table and Maurice took the bottle and expertly popped the cork. He poured a bit into my glass first. I tasted and nodded approval. Maurice filled all three glasses and said, "If that will be all . . ."

"No," I told him. "I want to talk to the owner. Julien Boisson."

Maurice got that troubled look again. "If you will tell me what it's about, I will inform Monsieur Boisson and . . ."

"It's for his ears only," I said, standing up. "I'll go with you." I nodded at Gauberti and Miol. "Drink and enjoy. I'll be back in a few minutes." I put a hand on Maurice's shoulder and gave a gentle push. "Let's go."

He led me reluctantly toward the rear of the disco.

We passed a dim side lounge and turned into a back hall-way that led to the bathrooms. Before we got to those, Maurice halted in front of a closed door with no sign on it. "Please," he said, "let me go in alone first and tell Monsieur Boisson you wish to see him. I don't want to lose this job."

"Go ahead," I told him.

"What name shall I give Monsieur Boisson?"

"Just say I want to see him."

Maurice sighed and knocked on the door. I heard the lock being turned inside. The door opened a scant six inches and a guy with the face of an unfriendly ape peered out. His build was apelike, too, straining his buttoned sport jacket. When he saw it was Maurice, he opened the door wider. Maurice went in and the door was shut.

I waited.

A slinky, leggy brunette in a silvery plastic micro dress that plunged to her belly button came out of the ladies' room. She eyed me speculatively as she strolled my way. I guessed what was in her gold beaded purse was the reason she'd gone in there. She had the hyper alert look they get after a snort of coke.

She started to pass me and then stopped and turned. "The music here always gets me so damned *hot*," she confided. "You, too?"

"Always."

She eyed me some more. "There's the side lounge—candlelight and soft couches? We could go cool each other down."

"I'm with someone."

"Me, too."

"Another night," I said.

"Party pooper." She grinned and wandered away.

The door of Julien Boisson's inner sanctum opened and Maurice stepped out. "Monsieur Boisson will see you," he told me before hurrying off along the hall, back to his work.

The ape in the strained sport jacket stood holding the door open, his unfriendly eyes memorizing my face. I went in past him. He closed the door and leaned his back against it, his gaze still fastened on me.

The room was more like an overfurnished sitting room than an office. The desktop was black marble, its polished shine reflecting the elaborate standing candelabras on either end of it. The walls were covered with tapestry. A white marble coffee table on black legs was flanked by two yellowing elephant tusks. The three easy chairs arranged around it had their seat cushions, arms, and backrests covered with flowered brocade. The chair behind the desk was covered in the same material.

The man standing beside it was about forty, wearing a white dinner jacket over a black shirt unbuttoned to show a couple thick gold chains hanging from his scrawny neck. He was skinny all over except for a potbelly. There was a blood-red carnation in his buttonhole, and his thin, hard-bitten face was decorated by a black handlebar mustache and two-pronged beard.

"Boisson?" I said.

"Yes. You didn't give Maurice your name. Perhaps for a reason?" He affected a stiffly cultivated manner of speech. He seemed more curious about me than worried. "If there is some difficulty, I have friends rather high up in both the Interior and Defense ministries." He gestured at a phone on the side table behind his desk. "I can call one of them and have him straighten you out, if you wish."

I told him my name.

His eyes narrowed. "You're not a cop."

His ape-man took a step away from the closed door and started to unbutton his jacket.

"No," I said, "but the two men with me *are* cops. They're expecting me to rejoin them in a few minutes. If I don't, they'll be in here asking why. They won't ask nicely. So warn your thug here not to try anything foolish."

Boisson looked at the ape-man and said softly, "No. Not with police in the house."

The ape-man stopped moving toward me. He stood there with his jacket opened but his gun undrawn. Boisson looked back to me. "What do you want?" he demanded angrily.

I strolled over to one of the easy chairs by the coffee table and sat down. Etienne Soulier's wallet was inside the left sleeve of my jacket where I'd put it before coming into the disco. I leaned back in the chair and rested my hands on my thighs and looked at Boisson. "You sent a couple guys to rough me up. I don't know why, but I surely don't like it."

Phoon Jamsai would have reported to Boisson by now that he'd been knocked out and had woken up later in an alley. He probably wouldn't remember anything at all about spilling his guts under the influence of Novak's drugs. If he did remember any of it, he was unlikely to tell his boss what he'd done.

"I don't know what you're talking about," Boisson said, not trying to make that sound sincere. "Who told you that I have anything to do with this—incident?"

"I have friends," I said vaguely. "I asked around. One of them pointed a finger." My tone abruptly sharpened: "If your thug pulls that gun, you're in big trouble!"

Boisson looked quickly at his ape-man, who looked back at him and complained in an aggrieved voice, "I didn't make a *move*."

When they looked at me again, my hands were back on my thighs. Mission accomplished. The wallet was under the seat cushion.

Boisson told me coldly, "Your friend was wrong."

"No, he wasn't." I let anger surface in my own voice. "And I don't take shit like that lying down. Those two cops waiting for me are friends, too. I don't want to get them in trouble. But I've got other friends who aren't cops and don't mind trouble. For themselves or anybody else. By noon I'll have contacted enough of them. We're going to come and wreck your joint. Teach you not to mess with me."

"Get out," Boisson grated.

"Sure," I said, and got to my feet. "Now that I've said what I came to say. Have a good sleep. But you'd better remove anything you care about that's breakable."

I walked toward the door. Boisson nodded. The ape-man opened it. As I moved past him he suddenly rammed the heel of his hand against the back of my shoulder, jolting me forward a step.

I recovered my balance and turned around to face him and said in English: "You raised in a barn?"

It confused him a little. "What?"

"That's American," I told him in French, "for didn't anybody ever teach you good manners?" On the last word I slapped him. Not hard. Lightly enough to be doubly insulting.

His face got red. Boisson snapped at him, "Don't!" But his ape-man wasn't listening. He came at me, moving pretty fast for his size. Not with his fists. The Thais must have taught him a few things. He drove his heel at my instep and a forearm at my nose.

I shifted my feet and his heel missed. I ducked under his forearm smash and took hold of his other wrist and elbow. I twisted him around and threw him across the hallway outside. He bounced off the wall there and came back at me.

I made a serious effort to reeducate him.

It took about fifteen seconds. When it was finished, I felt better and he didn't feel anything. I turned from his uncon-

scious hulk on the hallway carpet and looked back inside at
Boisson.

I smiled at him. "See you later."

26

I SET MY MENTAL ALARM FOR SEVEN-THIRTY THAT MORNING, which didn't give me enough sleep to face the world with too much enthusiasm. I forced my eyes half-open and carefully extricated myself from Arlette's bed-warmed arms and legs. She made soft sounds like she was eating one of her favorite rich desserts and continued to slumber. A hot-and-cold shower got my eyes fully opened but didn't clear all the sloth out of my head. When I put my bathrobe on, it smelled of Arlette. No help in my battle against returning to bed.

A bulldog courage I had to admire carried me to the kitchen instead. I made some very strong coffee and drank enough of it to get my voice and brain working. Refilling the cup, I carried it into my living room and phoned the apartment of Commissaire Jean-Claude Gojon of the B.R.I.—the Police Judiciaire's Brigade de Recherche et d'Intervention.

"I'm just about to head off to work," Gojon grumbled at the other end of the line.

That I knew. After some years of wary dealings with Commissaire Gojon, I could usually pinpoint what he would be up to at any hour around the clock. "I've got some hot information for you," I told him.

"I'm listening," he said, with all the warmth of a mosquito bite.

We got along like a cat and dog in the same household.

Without open hostility but without a whole lot of affection. Gojon was habitually suspicious of what I might be up to, and I worked at not giving him proof his suspicions were correct. But I'd also given him a number of tips in the past that had enhanced his reputation within the Police Judiciaire of the Paris area. So he heard me out. I told him about Julien Boisson and his association with a Bangkok-based criminal syndicate called the Midnight Sister Society.

Gojon had never heard about a gang using that name. He did know of Boisson and his disco. "Some wild goings on there, but he has enough protection to get away with that. There have been rumors Boisson is mob-connected, but no evidence of specific infractions."

"I've got a few specifics for you," I said. "Boisson uses the floor over Cozy's as a hideout for dangerous hoods. And some of them are illegal aliens. If you were to go in there, you'd find them carrying guns they don't have permits for. According to my information Boisson is also dealing coke. I've got a feeling a thorough search of his office will turn up proof of that."

"You've got a feeling, eh?"

"Strong feeling," I said. "Another thing. Boisson is expecting trouble from some rival gang. So move in cautiously because some of his hoods are bound to be on guard outside. And you'll have to move pretty fast—by this afternoon Boisson will probably have moved out evidence of everything you could use against him."

"I haven't said I'm ready to move on this," Gojon said thinly.

"It's a hot tip and I'm giving it to you instead of some other cop. Whether you cash in on it or not is up to you, naturally."

There was a short silence at the other end of the line. Then Gojon said, "If I go in there and your tip turns out wrong, I'll be in considerable trouble. If that happens, I'll see to it that you're in worse trouble."

"I know that, Commissaire. I wouldn't be calling you if I weren't sure."

"How sure?"

"Very."

There was another short silence. Then Gojon made a sound like clearing his throat of something unpleasant and hung up. I got dressed in jeans, turtleneck sweater, and a wool-lined car coat, holstered my Beretta to the back of my belt, and went out.

Two of the gunnies Alfani had rented were out in front of the courtyard entrance to the house and two more were watching the back alley behind it. I spoke briefly with one of them.

"A couple characters came by," he told me. "Around four this morning. Looking over the place. We asked what they wanted. They didn't say, but they went away."

"Good."

"They might come back, though. With reinforcements."

"I think," I said, "they're going to be too involved with their own problems to bother us much for a while."

I walked on to a bistro on Place de la Contrescarpe and had myself a big breakfast to make up for the hours of sleep I hadn't gotten. Little kids were scampering across the *place* on their way to school, escorted by their young mothers and an occasional grandparent. Some of the mothers were also pushing carriages with their new babies. The schoolkids were swinging their bookbags at one another and shouting friendly insults, full of morning energy. Normal life. The kind Christine Boyer had never known.

I picked up a couple fresh croissants from the *boulangerie* on the way back to my apartment. Arlette was up and showered, wearing my bathrobe while she had her coffee. I had offered to buy her a robe of her own, but she seemed to prefer using mine. I gave her the croissants. She dunked one in her coffee and gobbled it hungrily.

She paused before attacking the second one and said, "You look a little sleepy."

"You don't."

"I'm young," Arlette pointed out. "Age is creeping up on you."

"Thank you very much."

She grinned, dunked her second croissant, and told me her friend at *Jours de France* was contacting someone at *Paris-Match* about the original photograph of Christine Boyer they'd used. "When they find it, I'll go pick it up and get enlargements made of just the part with her face."

"Call Felix and Arnie and get them over here before you go out," I reminded her.

Arlette nodded. Her mouth was too full of croissant to speak. I glanced at my watch and said, "Fritz ought to be up by now."

Arlette finished swallowing and took a sip of coffee. "He's been up awhile. I've already told him about Christine being at that party thrown by Nicole de Scouarnac. Turns out Fritz has a better contact to her than I do. He knew her father—and her when she was a kid. He's phoning her place for an appointment to go see her."

"Good. If Fritz knows her, he's likely to get more out of her than I would." Things seemed to be moving nicely, between Arlette and Fritz—and what I hoped Commissaire Gojon was doing by now—without my pushing too much this morning. That was a relief because I was still feeling a little too groggy to push with much zeal myself. There were only two ways to cure that. Go back to sleep or take a swim.

I had my swimming trunks wrapped in a towel when I dropped into Fritz's place on my way out. "Nicole's sleeping late this morning," he told me. "I spoke to her social secretary. He said he'll give her my message after she's had her breakfast."

"Think she'll see you?"

Fritz seemed surprised by the question. "Why wouldn't she?"

"From her picture she looks too haughty to see anybody but God. And only if He made an appointment long in advance."

"The rich," Fritz said, "wear masks like the rest of us."

I left him waiting for the call and walked to Piscine Jean Taris on the other side of Place de la Contrescarpe.

I hate indoor swimming pools. Especially when it's not warm weather outside. Your body chemistry has to make violent adjustments coming and going. But if you want to stay tuned, you've got to move the blood around whatever way you can, and I hate jogging more than I hate indoor pools. A solid hour of doing laps at an unflagging pace bored hell out of me but did the job. I returned to the apartment with the last residue of sluggishness out of my system.

Arlette was gone and so was Fritz. She'd left a note telling me they'd gone off to their respective appointments. Her note ended with "Don't worry, Felix and Arnie are with me. I'll see they come to no harm."

I changed into flannel slacks and a fresh shirt and sweater. I was putting on socks and shoes when the phone rang. I picked up in the bedroom. The man calling said, "This Sawyer?"

I told him it was.

"You know who this is?" he asked.

"The voice is familiar," I said.

André Dédé Colin.

⊠ 27 ⊠

"YOU FOUND HER YET?" COLIN ASKED.

"I'm getting close," I told him. "I need a couple more days."

An edge of suspicion crept into his tone: "What's taking you so long?"

"If it were easy, you wouldn't need my help. You'd have located her yourself by now."

"I'm getting closer, too," Colin said warningly. "Real close."

"Bullshit. If you were, you wouldn't be calling to find out how I'm doing."

"I'm getting a feeling . . ." Colin said slowly. "Like you're jerking me around. Maybe trying to set me up."

"If that were what I was doing," I told him, "I'd have lied and said I've already found her. And have some people waiting to ambush you when you got to wherever I claimed she was."

I had thought of doing that. But finally decided against the try. Because Colin would almost certainly insist on speaking to her over the phone before believing me. When I did find Christine Boyer—when I could put her on the phone with him, proving I was playing it straight with him—*then* I could arrange the ambush.

He was silent so long I asked, "You still there?"

"I'm here. Okay—but *move* on it. We may be running out of time. Huang's got people hunting her, too."

"How do you know?"

"Never mind how. I just know."

"That means we may have to move fast when I do locate her," I said. "Waiting till you get around to calling me could be a fatal delay. If I knew where to reach you—or at least leave a message for you—it would be a smarter arrangement."

"Smarter for you," Colin said. "Not for me. We'll go on doing it my way."

I hung up after he did, and then slowly finished putting on my shoes. After that I sat there and worried about how Colin knew Huang's men were out searching for Christine Boyer.

The phone rang again. This time it was Commissaire Gojon.

"How'd you make out at Cozy's?" I asked him.

"Your tip was good," Gojon said grudgingly. "We took six men with guns they don't have permits for. Three of them aliens carrying forged papers."

"I wouldn't have given you the tip if it wasn't good," I said blandly.

"You were right about them being braced for trouble, too. We arrested two of them on watch outside the building. The other four inside. Two of those tried to shoot their way out. We had to kill one when one of mine was wounded. After that the rest surrendered."

"What about Julien Boisson?"

"He's in custody, too. Boisson claims he didn't know any of those men in his building had guns or were illegals. But that's not the only charge he's being held on."

"Ah," I said, "you did find coke in his office."

"No, we didn't," Gojon told me evenly. "But what we did find is even more interesting. A wallet belonging to a man who was murdered in the Sentier area last night. Tortured and drowned in his own bathtub. Boisson is being kept under *garde à vue* while we investigate his connection with that murder.''

"What do you know," I said, "you hit even luckier than I expected."

"Boisson swears he never saw that wallet. He says *some-one* must have planted it in his office."

"What else would you expect him to say? He's lying, of course."

"Of course," Gojon agreed dryly. He went on in the same tone: "At the moment, Sawyer, I am being praised by my superiors and envied by my peers. So you have done me a favor. Don't let that go to your head. I don't know what game you're playing, but I'm quite sure you are not playing it by the rules. Get too reckless and my gratitude will evaporate. I'll step on you like a bug."

"I always know I can count on you, Commissaire, to do the right thing." This time I managed to hang up before he did.

I found myself smiling, just a little. The loss of Boisson and his six thugs cut down the manpower Huang had available to him. Between that and his having to devote some hasty effort to repairing the damage to his organization, Huang wasn't going to be able to give as much as before to other pressing matters for a while. If he didn't have Christine Boyer yet, I still had a chance.

Neither Fritz nor Arlette had called me by noon. I turned on my answering machine, went out to the *place* for an early lunch, and finished it without dawdling. I was walking back to my place when one of Alfani's rented gunnies watching the front got out of his car and intercepted me.

His partner was standing against the wall nearby, eyeing a black BMW sedan that had parked there. His hands were inside his coat pockets. The one who'd climbed out of the car didn't have his hands in his pockets. But his coat was unbuttoned all the way, and when he turned to face me, it flared just enough to give me a flash of the stubby repeating shotgun hanging down his side from a string looped over his shoulder.

"There are three Oriental guys in that BMW," he told me. "One of them says he wants to talk to you. The other two look to me like guns."

I made sure my jacket was open enough for quick access to my Beretta before walking on to the BMW. The rented gunnie followed, drifting a little to the left so I wouldn't be in his line of fire if it came to shooting. His partner detached himself from the wall and moved to my right.

Huang was alone in the backseat. The other two were in the front seat. I bent enough to look inside as Huang wound down his window. "Only two bodyguards this time?" I said to him. "You getting less security-conscious or just cutting down on your overhead?"

"I seem to have underestimated you, Monsieur Sawyer," Huang said calmly. "I should have contacted you sooner. But I failed to realize your potential. My error."

"I like the way you put that—my potential."

Huang nodded, politely expressionless. "Yes, potential. For either interference or assistance. If I had realized, I would have offered to hire you much sooner."

"Hire me for what?" I asked, as expressionless as Huang. "To replace your loss of other employees?"

Huang permitted himself a fractional smile. "Something like that. I assume you have a living to earn. And that a larger income is preferable to a small one."

"I like money," I conceded.

"As do we all, Monsieur Sawyer. Won't you get in the car while we discuss this?"

"I think not. You can come up to my place with me. Just leave these two in the car."

Huang glanced at the gunnies standing to either side of me and shook his head regretfully. "It will be a short discussion.

We can continue it this way—if bending like that isn't too much of a strain on your back."

"My chiropractor tells me I have an unusually strong spine," I assured him.

"What I'm offering," Huang said, "is thirty thousand francs. For information that helps me to find either Dédé Colin or Christine Boyer. Does that interest you?"

"I like money," I repeated.

"I am prepared to pay it immediately—for the information."

"Unfortunately I don't have that information available yet."

"Then you will be paid when you do have it," Huang said, allowing only a sliver of disappointment to show.

"No down payment?"

Another fractional smile. "Forgive me, Monsieur Sawyer, but no. It does no harm to offer you an incentive and hope it will influence you—but, to be honest, I don't place much faith in your cooperation. Also I must advise you that the offer will be canceled if I obtain the information through other channels before you deliver. As I have reason to believe will happen, since you say you don't have the information yourself yet."

"How do I contact you when I get it?"

"I will contact you," Huang said, echoing Colin. He reached forward and poked his driver's shoulder with a plump finger. The car pulled away.

I was beginning to feel like an undesirable date. Nobody wanted to tell me where he lived.

⊠ 28 ⊠

THERE WAS A MESSAGE ON MY ANSWERING MACHINE FROM Fritz, giving me a number to call. I switched off the machine and dialed it. The man who answered said he was Nicole de Scouarnac's social secretary. I gave him my name and asked for Fritz. He asked me to please stay on the line while he put me through to Madame de Scouarnac's Winter Room.

It was a woman's voice that came on first. A neutral voice, neither warm nor cold, giving away nothing but overcultivated composure. "Monsieur Sawyer?"

"Yes. Madame de Scouarnac?"

"This is she. Please wait a moment. Fritz is coming to the phone."

First-name basis. Either her picture didn't do her justice or Fritz's way with women was thawing the ice queen.

Fritz came on the line sounding cheerful. "Nicole has been kind enough to invite me to lunch. Her cook is superb."

"Were you able to get her to open up before feeding you?"

"No problem, Peter. I knew Nicole when she was only a spoiled child. She can't put on airs with me now that she's become a spoiled though beautiful woman."

There was a burst of almost girlish laughter close to Fritz. He *did* have a way with them.

"First point of information," Fritz said. "Christine Boyer was *not* one of the guests at Nicole's party. She was one of

159

the waitresses. Nicole dressed all of those alike, in that sailor outfit.''

"If she was there as an employee, your Madame de Scouarnac must have hired her illegally. Christine Boyer always worked black. No papers.''

"As a matter of fact Christine wasn't the only one working black at that party. Like many of the rich, Nicole resents a social security system that tries to shift even an infinitesimal part of her wealth to those less fortunate.''

"I realize that the fact she's breaking the law probably doesn't worry her much,'' I said. "She's too important ever to get prosecuted for something like that. But it still leaves her open to pressure, if she's reluctant about anything we want to know. She might not like gossip columns revealing she's too cheap to pay for her employees' welfare and health insurance.''

"I have already pointed that out,'' Fritz told me lightly. "Nicole seems titillated by the idea of my blackmailing her. She says she's never had the experience before.''

There was a female chuckle near Fritz. I was glad it was he who' 'one to interrogate Nicole de Scouarnac. I was beginning to think I couldn't have handled it.

"How did she hire Christine?'' I asked.

"Through another waitress she'd used at other parties. A woman named Pascale Doya. Nicole needed extras for her New Year's affair. Pascale Doya brought Christine Boyer. But Nicole was extremely displeased by the way our Christine behaved and never employed either of them again.''

"What did Christine do that was so bad?''

"According to Nicole, she flirted outrageously with a number of the male guests. Not the sort of comportment Nicole expects of her employees.''

I could hear Nicole de Scouarnac muttering angrily, but I couldn't make out the words. I said, "Including the guy in the picture with her?''

"That seems to have been as much his fault as Christine's," Fritz said. "He's a struggling young sculptor that Nicole was encouraging at the time. Marc Viano. A photographer covering the party was about to take his picture when Christine walked by. Viano grabbed her and pulled her into the picture."

"That's not exactly flirting."

"Nicole feels Christine could have resisted if she had cared to. But she admits Viano was to blame, too. He'd been drinking too much—as he often did in spite of Nicole's efforts to make him cut down on it. She says that's why she finally dropped him from the group of aspiring artists she helps."

"He does look drunk in the picture," I said, "but he also looks damn pleased to be holding Christine. He just might have seen some more of her after that party. Be worth checking on him to find out."

"I've already done the preliminary checking on him," Fritz told me smoothly. "Nicole was kind enough to let me use her library phone and give me the number of the small hotel where he lived. I learned that Marc Viano isn't there anymore. They don't know where he moved to. I've called a number of friends in the art world. They say he wasn't managing to make a dent on Paris and he quit the city sometime last year. None of my contacts so far have heard anything about where he went."

"Now that is interesting," I said.

"Yes, isn't it. I'll continue to check on that one."

"What about other men at the party that Christine's supposed to have flirted with?"

"Nicole feels it wouldn't be nice of her to embarrass them by giving us any of their names. I don't believe that even our blackmail will move her from that position."

I thought I heard another chuckle in the background. "That leaves the waitress who brought Christine to the party," I said. "We should be able to track her down."

"I've already done that, too," Fritz told me. "Pascale Doya used to work at a restaurant Nicole frequents. The patron still had the phone number of her apartment. I got her husband there. He says she's at the crêperie they own." Fritz gave me the address. "You can follow up on that while I get back to Nicole's splendid lunch and delightful company."

He was beginning to sound like the Fritz Donhoff I had always known. Mind, charm, and energy all back on Go. You don't have to be Chinese to perk up on Dr. Lu's magic elixir.

◪ 29 ◪

IT WAS ON AVENUE D'ITALIE, BETWEEN A BRASSERIE CALLED
Le Levant and a bar called Le Sahara. Near the edge of
Chinatown—but I didn't know if that had any significance.
The interior was narrow and shallow, with the counter on
one side and a line of small tables on the other. Your typical
Parisian working-class neighborhood crêperie. What wasn't
typical was the artwork decorating it. Paintings on the walls
and two sculptures, one in wood and the other in colored
plaster, at the ends of the counter.

Except for a woman cleaning up between the lunch and
dinner rushes the place was empty. The woman gestured at
the big hot plates behind the counter. "Can't give you anything to eat for another hour. They're all turned off."

I nodded at the espresso machine. "That working?" She
said it was. I asked for a small café noir. While she made it,
I sat on a counter stool and watched her. She was in her
thirties, a pretty woman with a chunky build. Wearing a
stained apron over sweatshirt and dungarees. When she put
the coffee in front of me, I asked if she was Pascale Doya.
She nodded and I said, "You're a friend of Christine Boyer's."

Her smile was instant and warm. "Christine ask you to
drop by and say hello? How is she?"

"I don't know. I'm trying to find her for an attorney. A

163

distant uncle died and left her a little money in his will." An old wheeze but it almost always works. It happens often enough in reality so that few people question it.

"Oh," Pascale Doya said, disappointed. "Well, I can't help you. No idea where she is these days. I haven't seen Christine since . . . oh, more than two years ago."

"How well did you know her?"

"She used to come here for lunch or dinner a lot. Starting back when I just worked here part-time. Before I married my husband. He owns this place. Christine and I started talking to each other after she'd been in a few times and we got to like each other."

"She ever tell you where she was from?"

"Sure—that's how we began talking. She had an accent I couldn't place, so I asked her. She was born and raised in Indochina. Christine's mother and father were French, but they were living over there when she was born."

I decided Christine's small lie didn't mean anything except as part of her desire to *belong* in France. "Where was she living when you knew her?"

Pascale Doya shrugged that she didn't know. "Some dump, she said. She said she was going to move someplace nicer as soon as she made enough dough to afford it. How'd you find out I used to know Christine?" There was no suspicion in the question, only curiosity.

"From Nicole de Scouarnac," I told her.

"*That* bitch." Pascale Doya made a disgusted face. "She got mad at both of us—just because a good-looking artist *she* had the hots for got more interested in Christine."

I took out the clipping from *Paris-Match* and showed it to her. "The man in this picture?"

"That's him. Marc Viano. Where did you get this?"

"It was among some things Christine left behind, one of the places she lived."

"I'm surprised she didn't take it with her. I remember when Christine cut that out of the magazine. My God, she was hot for Marc. And he was crazy about her.'' Pascale Doya's expression took on a soft romanticism as she looked at the picture again. ''And that's where it started, at that party.''

''They went on seeing each other.''

''Sure—and Marc, he was stupid enough to admit it to Madame de Scouarnac. He was one of her protégés—that was practically his only source of income. And she quit helping him when she found out he was seeing Christine.''

''She says she dropped him because he drank too much.''

''He did, though that's not why she dropped him. Marc's drinking—that was because he wasn't making out in his career. *I* think he's a great sculptor. So does my husband. That's how we came to start this collection here. Christine brought Marc around a few times, and my husband felt sorry for him because he was so broke. So we bought something from him, and after that we got interested in art.''

Pascale Doya pointed to the sculpture on one end of the counter. ''That's his.''

It was about a foot tall, carved out of olive wood, partly abstract and partly intertwined male and female nudes.

''It is good,'' I said.

''Everybody comes in here likes it. But Marc hardly ever managed to sell any of his work. So he'd start brooding over that and get drunk. Christine thought maybe if she moved in with him she could make him stop that. But she never did because she left Paris.''

Pascale Doya shook her head sadly. ''I remember when she came in here to say good-bye. Looking like she wanted to cry but not letting herself. I think she was really in love with Marc. But she said she had to go away. She wouldn't say why or where she was going. Just that she *had* to. That was when I told you I last saw her—more than two, maybe three years ago.''

The timing made it when Huang had forced Christine

Boyer to move up to Antwerp. After his partner, Streuvels, had fallen for her.

I gestured at the olive wood sculpture. "Know where I could find Marc Viano?"

"No. He came by a couple times after Christine left. In bad shape. Asking if we'd heard anything about where she'd gone. But then he stopped coming. The last time he was in he was saying he ought to move out to the country somewhere, get far away from all the phonies of the Paris art world. Maybe he did."

"And you never heard from Christine again."

"Nothing," Pascale Doya said, "except a postcard once, a few months ago."

I said quietly, "Where did she send it from?"

"I don't know. Nothing on it that says where." She pointed to a dozen picture postcards tacked together on the door to the back storeroom. "Sometimes our regulars send us those when they go on trips. Christine's is the one with the fishes."

"I'd like to look at it."

Pascale Doya unfastened one of the postcards and brought it to me.

The picture side of it was of seven different kinds of florid-colored, strikingly patterned tropical fish.

On the other side the message was written with a ballpoint pen: "Dear Pascale—I am happy now. Hope you still are. With love, Christine."

Two descriptive lines printed on that side of the card had been scratched out. The stamp had been stuck to the picture side, where it was impossible to read the postmark.

But I knew that card. I had seen enough of them on the sales racks in the past. The postage stamp Christine had used was French, but the tropical fish pictured on the card weren't in a French aquarium. They were in the Oceanographic Museum in Monaco.

Back in my own backyard.

⊠ **30** ⊠

I SPENT THAT EVENING AND ALL THE NEXT DAY DOWN IN Monaco, prowling around with my picture of Christine Boyer. The close-up of her face that Arlette had gotten made from the photo used by *Paris-Match*. I explained that the girl in the picture would look three years older now. She might also have changed the style and even the color of her hair. Most people were cooperative. They studied the photograph carefully before deciding they didn't know her. A few said they might have seen her at some time but that they could be mistaken.

One problem was that Christine was a type—there were too many her age who looked sort of like her. Several times I saw one and hurried closer before being sure it wasn't Christine. Once the resemblance was so close I stopped the look-alike and questioned her, only to discover she was a Swedish student on holiday.

I didn't often lapse into going about it that haphazardly. A methodical search needs a point of departure, a frame of reference. If you're looking for a physical fitness freak, you show his picture around the local gyms and bodybuilding equipment shops. If your quarry is an auto mechanic, you check with all the repair garages. What I had on Christine Boyer was that she'd worked as a waitress in the past. Most of my first evening and second day were spent checking out restaurants, bars, and brasseries.

There was nothing wrong with that system—if Christine Boyer was in or near Monaco. It was no good at all if she lived too far away to come in for more than an occasional visit. Or if she was in Spain or Denmark and had sent that postcard the only time she'd ever passed through Monaco. The hordes of tourists I kept seeing during my prowl were a sobering reminder of that possibility.

I didn't confine the search to Monaco. There were a couple local private investigators I'd hired to canvass Menton and Nice with copies of Christine's picture. Those were the closest big communities east and west of Monaco. I checked by phone with them at regular intervals. They didn't make out any better than I did with the approach based on Christine having worked as a waitress.

I shifted to another logical approach. She had been nuts about a sculptor named Marc Viano. I hit art galleries with her picture—and Viano's, taken from the same magazine photo of them. My hired P.I.s did the same in Nice and Menton. So did Fritz and Arlette as part of their hunt for Marc Viano up in Paris. By the end of my second night in Monaco none of us had come up with a lead.

I went at it again early the next morning using a different reasonable method. Few people in and around France tolerate packaged bread with preservatives. They buy fresh-baked bread. Every day. So I took my picture of Christine to *boulangeries*. Most people on the Riviera drive cars and have to get them refueled regularly. I hit the gas stations. At eleven that morning I'd tried all the *boulangeries* and gas stations and drawn another blank.

I decided to call it quits for a few hours. Disconnect the logic sectors of the brain. Hope the disorganized subconscious would cast up something new I could work with.

I drove home and went down to the cove below it for a

swim. When I was a long way out to sea, I rolled over and floated on my back. Concentrating on not concentrating.

It was a lot easier to do there than at a crowded Champs-Élysées tourist trap. The long heavy swells raised and lowered me with a slow hypnotic rhythm. I gazed lazily at the sky. Only a few wisps of cloud up there, very high. I watched them gradually shredding apart as they drifted past.

''She's with the goats. . . .''

Kukrit Chaudee was the one who had said that. The former monk and soothsayer from Thailand. He'd said it and then admitted he couldn't explain it.

Oriental mysticism on a belly full of Big Mac. Forget it.

I rose and fell with the sea. A little cloud began to materialize up there where none had been before.

Was I making any progress with my sensible approaches to finding Christine Boyer? I was not.

I swam back to the cove, climbed to the house, and got dressed. I drove back to Monaco and went to the Condamine market. All the food vendors were closing up their stands for the day, but none of them had left yet.

I began showing Christine Boyer's picture to the ones who sold local goat cheese.

⊠ **31** ⊠

I drove up past the highest of the Riviera's three corniche roads and on into the harsh, sparsely inhabited hinterland beyond the Col d'Eze.

Above the pass I took a narrow road that twisted its way into a chaos of stony hills and eroded ravines. The first mile of sharp bends had a few boarded-up weekend houses and some stretches of woods. But as the road climbed, the landscape became increasingly bleak and empty. Mine was the only car moving through it.

The dense forest that once covered these hills was long gone. Destroyed by wind-whipped fires. What was left was rugged terrain of weathered white rocks with clumps of weeds and tangles of scrub brush growing out of the thin soil between them.

The air up there was pure and sharp. It took a little getting used to. So did an utter silence broken only by the sound of crickets.

Atop some high ridges there were views of the sea and the Côte d'Azur far below. What I was driving through was a different world. It belonged more to the view in the other direction, where snow still clung to bare peaks of the distant Alps.

Both views abruptly disappeared when I was up at about two thousand feet. My car had entered a big patch of hill fog. What it really is, that kind of fog, is a cloud pasting itself around a hilltop. Inside it all I could see was what was close to the road. Outcrops of bulging stone slid by. Black skeletons of burned trees materialized and vanished in the white blur.

When I came out of it, into afternoon sunlight without a trace of mist, I was at the place where I'd been told to take a side road to the left.

The turnoff was just before a broken-walled, roofless barrack. It had once belonged to Fort de la Revère, closed and abandoned years ago. The main fort had been built as the hub of a tunnel system leading under a dozen surrounding hills to outlying bunkers, observation posts, and gun emplacements. It had never served any practical use except as a military prison in World War II.

I couldn't see the fort where I turned into the side road. But I knew it well. From my summers on the coast below when I was in my teens. Coming up there with others and finding ways to get into the old fort and explore its forbidden underground passages.

The side road curved around the slope of a massive hill and under an artillery cupola. Built of reinforced concrete sunk deep inside the slope, and covered with earth overgrown by wild bushes, nothing of it showed except the long, thin slit of its gunport. After that was left behind the surface of the road deteriorated. It became a succession of deep ruts and potholes. Difficult, slow driving. Worse where it became not much wider than the car, with a naked cliff rising on one side and a long drop on the other.

Then the drop shallowed and narrowed. Became a ravine. The road crossed it via a broad shoulder, to the side of a second hill.

The going got easier there. The ground along the other slope was wider, skirting the remains of an incinerated grove of big pines. The road became a dirt track covered fairly recently with a loose layer of crushed stones.

But I didn't like it. According to my Peugeot's kilometrage indicator I was getting near where I was going—and the noise of my tires on that surface would carry too far. I pulled off the track on a high hump and parked among the gaunt, dark corpses of the pines. Then I dug into the hidden compartment inside the backseat.

The gun I kept tucked away in this car was a Heckler & Koch P7. I slipped it into the right-hand pocket of my jacket. I already had a Beretta holstered under the jacket, but an extra pistol might be a lifesaver. Huang and company could already be there. Or Colin.

From the glove compartment I took a pair of binoculars. Smaller than my open hand, but with high-powered lenses. I put that in the left pocket of my jacket.

There was a keen wind cutting through the high ravine. It stirred up dust along the road I had traveled. I could see a long way back from where I stood beside the car. No other vehicle was coming after me along that road.

I couldn't see as far ahead. The graveled track bent around the side of the second hill there. I proceeded on foot with all due caution. Going through the dead grove. Keeping away from the track but following its direction around the hill.

There the track diverted from a wide ledge, turned back on itself, and descended into a big hollow surrounded by hills. I crouched low on the ledge and eased to its edge. I leaned forward just enough to see the bottom of the hollow where the track ended.

The terrain was a bit softer down there. Sheltered from the full force of winds and wind-driven rain. There was a small stockade and several buildings. One was a big, green Quonset hut. Probably used for keeping the goats when they were not out grazing, and for milking them. Next to it was a much smaller building that had to be a smokehouse for turning the goats' milk into marketable cheeses. The main house had been one of Fort de la Revère's outlying barracks. Its walls had been patched, plastered, and painted a dull brick-red. It had a roof of new orange-colored tiles.

I got out the binoculars and studied the buildings through them. Some shade trees had been planted around the main house. Which meant lugging in enough good rich dirt to plant them in. Pines and fast-growing willows and eucalyptus. There was a bench and a picnic-type wooden table to one side of the front door. On the other side was a large block of stone. And next to that a stone statue. Part abstract, with the nude of a slim woman escaping from the rest of it—dancing or trying to fly, I couldn't be sure which. In spite of being made of stone the style was the same as the wooden sculpture in the crêperie in Paris.

What I didn't see was anybody at all around the buildings. Someone—or more than one—could be inside them. But there was no car down there.

I used the binoculars for a slow, careful scan of the surrounding slopes. The biggest and most gradual slope—actually a series of interlocked ones with a lot of scrub brush—was behind the buildings. Rising to the hilltop that held Fort de la Revère. I couldn't see it, but I knew it was up there. The shape of that hill was familiar from the past.

I still hadn't seen anybody. Lowering the binoculars, I gave my eyes a rest for a few minutes. Then I heard the tinkling of a bell coming from a cleft between two small hills off to the right of the hollow. I looked in that direction. Several more minutes passed before the source of the tinkling appeared out of the cleft. A string of twenty goats, with the bell around the neck of the one in the lead.

They took their time, pausing to munch at wild bushes. Sage and lavender, mint and thyme. The cheese from their milk would have that mixture of lovely flavor.

A small, slender young woman was shepherding the goats toward the green Quonset hut. She didn't have to work at it too hard. A big mongrel dog was eagerly taking care of most of it for her. Running back and forth to bark at any goat that strayed. I focused the binoculars on the woman.

It was her—Christine Boyer.

She wore flat-heeled work boots, patched dungarees, and a heavy sweater. Over that a short opened coat made of goat-skins stitched together. Homemade. Waste not, want not.

She *had* changed in three years. Not all the change was due to aging. Her face was fuller, stronger, with new lines in it that gave it character. Her figure was sturdier. She looked solid, competent, more mature than her twenty years.

I put the binoculars back in my pocket and watched her shoo the goats into the Quonset hut. As she shut the door on them, I started down the near slope, my shoes crunching ground-clinging brush that exuded tangy fragrances.

The dog heard my approach first. It spun to face me, legs spread, growling. But not in preparation for attack. It was an efficient shepherd, with no real ferocity in its nature.

Alerted by her dog, Christine looked around and saw me coming toward her. She twisted away and sprinted to the house, shoved open the door, and dodged inside.

I took some long fast strides and flattened my back against the front wall next to the door.

She came out with a rifle. A single-shot .22. It was held ready in both hands, but she couldn't spot where I was for a moment. Long enough. I reached out a hand and snatched the rifle away from her.

She reached inside her open coat and yanked a mean-looking knife from a belt sheath. She pointed it at me threat-eningly, not quite prepared to use it on me unless I made it necessary for her to defend herself.

"Who are you?" she demanded hoarsely.

"I'm here to help you," I said, "not harm you." I drew the Beretta from the holster under my jacket. Her eyes went wide and she drew back half a step. I reversed the pistol and held it out to her butt-first. ''Here, this will make you feel more secure than the knife.''

Christine reached out hesitantly with her free hand, ready for a trick. When I simply went on holding the gun out to her, she took it from me. After a moment, still uncertain, she sheathed the knife and kept the pistol aimed at me, finger across the trigger.

WHEN SHE DIDN'T TRY TO SQUEEZE THE TRIGGER, I TOLD her, "The safety's on."

"What?"

"It won't shoot if you don't take the safety off."

Christine Boyer looked down at the gun in her hand. "I—don't know how."

"Good." I leaned the .22 rifle against the wall and sat on the edge of the wooden table. Trying to relax her by acting relaxed myself. I wasn't. I wanted to get her out of there. But I needed her cooperation for that. Quickly and briefly I told her about myself and Arlette Alfani, Colin, and Huang. She listened, but her scowl was suspicious.

I gestured at the stone statue. "Marc Viano still have that drinking problem?"

She started to give a negative shake of her head, then stopped herself.

"Why isn't he here?" I asked her.

"You expect me to trust you, but you still haven't told me any reason why I should."

"Lee To Hyun trusts me," I said. "The man from Korea who rescued you from that refugee boat in the Thailand Gulf after your mother was killed. He trusts me and I think you trust him."

176

Her scowl was still suspicious. "How do you know about him and . . ." She didn't finish it.

"A good friend of his, Dr. Lu, introduced us. Can you read French?"

The sudden question puzzled her. "I can now. Slowly—but I can read."

I took out my wallet and opened to my professional ID, and held it out for her to look at. She studied it, frowning. "You're a detective."

"Private."

"Maybe Colin paid you to find me for him."

I nodded at my pistol in her hand. "Then I wouldn't have given you that." While she considered that I said, "You seem more afraid of Colin than of Huang. That's a mistake. I don't think Colin wants to hurt you."

"He'll hurt *Marc*."

"Why do you think so?"

"He killed Streuvels in Antwerp because he wanted me," Christine said. "If he still wants me, he'll kill Marc." Her guard was coming down. "I don't understand what you said about Huang. I've always been afraid he would come after me—but to avenge my telling the police about Colin."

"No—Huang wants the jewels from the Antibes robbery."

"But I don't have them. I don't know where they are."

"If that's true," I told her, "it would surprise me." After watching her expression, I added: "Maybe you do but don't realize it. We can talk that over later. Right now we've got to get you someplace safe." I gestured with my opened wallet. "You see my name and my picture confirms it is mine. If you still have doubts about me, call your friend Lee."

"We don't have a phone here."

"We'll make the call from Eze. My car's around the other side of the hill."

"I can't just go. Marc will come back, and if he's here

when *they* come—Colin or Huang—I can't let Marc face that alone."

"Where is he?"

This time she answered the question: "With his uncle. His uncle is the one who knows all about goats and cheese making. He's been helping us get started here. Teaching us. But he has back trouble. Marc took him to the doctor in Nice."

"When's their appointment?"

Christine looked at her watch. "About now."

"We'll call the doctor's office from Eze. Tell them to meet us instead of coming back here."

"But what if they've left the doctor's office before we can get them on the phone and warn them?"

"Then I'll come back here and get them away," I told her. "But first *we've* got to get away. I'm not coming back without reinforcements. I've got to recruit some—and fast."

Christine Boyer studied me a moment longer. Then she gave me back my pistol.

She told me some of it while she made sure the goats were all right in their shed and tethered her dog to a long line where it could reach bowls of food and water. She told me about Huang forcing her to move to Antwerp—to work in his Bangkok Bar and be his partner's mistress.

"Huang introduced Streuvels to me one evening when they were in Paris together. Streuvels took me to dinner and a disco called Cozy's. And he—wanted me. I didn't like him at all, and I certainly didn't want to go to Antwerp with him. I was already falling in love with Marc. But I had no choice. Huang made that plain—that he wouldn't let me refuse."

She said it without self-pity. Nor even any show of anger. As if being forced to quit a man she loved for one she disliked was a disagreeable but not surprising fact of life. The kind she had learned too early to expect and accept because it couldn't be escaped, only survived.

"And in Antwerp you met Colin," I said, "and he got rid of Streuvels for you."

"He came into the Bangkok Bar one night with Huang. I served them. Huang saw Colin liked me. He went to his back room and left us alone together. He told me to stay with Colin and forget about serving anybody else. I didn't know who or what Colin was at the time. We talked. He seemed kind and gentle. There was nothing to warn me he was mad. I told him how much I missed Paris. Though not about Marc, of course."

"This was before the Antibes robbery," I interrupted.

"Yes, but I didn't know anything about that then. Only that he was associated with Huang in some sort of project. Later Colin told me it was the Antibes robbery. He didn't tell me any details, though. Colin is not a man who needs to talk much. About anything."

"How soon after Antibes did he come for you?"

"Less than a week later. Colin was waiting for me outside the bar one night after I finished work. He told me Streuvels was dead and he was going to take me to Paris with him. He didn't ask if I wanted to go with him. I didn't care for him—not in the way he expected me to. But after I understood he had murdered Streuvels, I was too scared of him to argue much.

"He didn't even give me time to pack my things. He had a car waiting and he put me in it and drove us down to Paris. He had already rented an apartment there for us."

Christine told me the rest while we climbed the graveled track toward my car.

"Colin warned me that Huang was after him as well as the police. He told me never to mention his name to anybody. We seldom went anywhere together. Sometimes he went out alone, at night. Several times he was away for a few days, I don't know where. He kept a great deal of money in the apartment and he always gave me more than enough of it to spend any way I wanted when he was away. He wasn't interested in what I did while he was gone, as long as I was there for him when he came back.''

"So you went to see Marc Viano again.''

"Yes—and realized I was still in love with him. Marc's drinking had gotten worse while I was in Antwerp. But he knew he had to stop that. Before it reached the stage where he couldn't stop, and died of it. He thought if he could move far away from Paris it would help. If he could live in the country somewhere, cheaply, and earn his living at something other than sculpture.

"And he talked to me about his uncle, and spending a lot of his childhood with him. His uncle knows everything about raising goats and making cheese from their milk. That is his métier. But a few years ago all his goats got a sickness and died. He didn't have the money—or the youth—to start over again.

"It was Marc's dream that he would somehow raise enough money to go into that business with his uncle. Then he could be more patient about developing himself as an artist. Without the pressure of trying to sell what he did immediately. He could make enough with the goats, and work at his sculpture at the same time, and wait out however many years it took for the art world to discover him.

"But,'' Christine added quietly, "Marc said he knew he would never have the strength of character to do it—unless I went with him.''

"So you told the police how to catch Colin.''

"I had to,'' Christine said. Without any troubled conscience. For her it was simply another fact of life she'd had to accept. "I was afraid if I just ran away, Colin would come after me and kill Marc. I thought the police would put him away so that could never happen. But now he's out. And searching for me, like I was frightened he would.''

"He's after the Antibes jewels,'' I said.

"But I don't have them.''

"Where did you get enough money to start this goat farm?"

"The money Colin kept in the apartment," Christine told me. "I took it all, the same time I informed on Colin to the police. It was just enough to buy the first goats and rent this piece of land. The rent is cheap. It's government property, and not good for anything else."

"Stealing Colin's money didn't bother you," I said, "but you didn't take his jewel loot."

"It wasn't in the apartment. Colin never said where he hid it." There was a brief flash of anger from her. "That's the truth, damn it! I don't know about any jewels and I don't *care* about them. We don't need that kind of money. We're doing well here. The government says it's prepared to sell us the land—whenever we save enough to make the down payment. And we will, given time."

"If we can get Colin and Huang off your back," I said.

She was silent for a time as we trudged around the bend in the graveled track. Then she said quietly: "Yes."

We were a few steps from my car when I saw the cloud of dust rising on the road that curved in our direction along the slope of the opposite hill. It wasn't the kind of dust stirred up by wind.

A black car emerged from it. I got the binoculars and took a close-up look. It was a BMW sedan. Same license plate as the one that had parked in front of my apartment in Paris, waiting for me. I sharp-focused on the men inside the car.

Huang and crew. He was back to traveling with his normal quota of goons. Four of them.

☒ **33** ☒

I GAVE CHRISTINE A SHOVE TOWARD MY PEUGEOT. "ALL aboard. It's Huang."

She was in the front seat shutting her door before I swung in behind the wheel and started the motor. The car was already aimed in the right direction—away from Huang's oncoming BMW. I drove out of the fire-gutted woods onto the graveled track and headed around the bend.

"This doesn't lead to any way out," Christine said, tensed but not terrified. "It ends at our place."

"It'll have to do."

We had one temporary advantage. The potholed road the BMW was still on made for slow going. The graveled track we were using was much faster. A few more minutes' lead could make the difference.

I drove down the track into the hollow and raced on past the buildings. Nearing the big slopes behind them I shifted into second gear and rammed the accelerator to the floor, asking the Peugeot for all the power it could muster. It bucked its way up the first slope, smashing through bushes, skidding, ripping its sides against spurs of jutting rock.

I told Christine to get the flashlight out of the glove compartment. It was a small, flat one with a hinged handle. She slid it into her coat pocket as the car scrunched and whined over the crest of the lowest slope. We bounced down into a dip behind it and then roared up the next slope.

We were about halfway up that one when the Peugeot stalled and began to roll back down. I yanked the hand brake, jumped out, and looked back.

The black BMW was coming down the track into the hollow below.

Christine was out of the Peugeot beside me. I snapped, "Let's go," and we charged up the hill on foot.

When the enemy outnumbers you, the best defense is to run away. Any animal knows that. It's built into the survival instinct. The four Huang had with him looked young and fit. Able to move fast. But if we could stay ahead of them until we got over the top of the hill—past Fort de la Revère—there were areas down the slopes on the other side where I knew we could lose the pursuit.

I looked back down again. Huang and his goon squad were out of the BMW. Huang was empty-handed, but the goons were not. One had a shotgun, another carried what looked like an Uzi submachine gun, and two had rifles. They started up the slopes after us.

I motioned to Christine. She didn't understand at first. Most of my wind was going into moving fast up a steepening incline, but I got the words out: "Get behind me—and stay close."

She obeyed immediately, dropping back just enough to shield my back. That was better. They weren't going to shoot at me with her in that position. Too much chance of hitting her. Huang wouldn't like it if she got killed before he had a chance to interrogate her—or to use her as bait for Colin.

It seemed like a good idea, but the next second I knew it wasn't.

A bullet whipped between my knees. It slashed through a big myrtle bush a few feet ahead of me, pulverized a barb of limestone, and ricocheted off to the right. The shot still echoed when I reached back a hand, seized the front of

Christine's goatskin coat, and threw us both down into a shallow dip behind a heavy growth of wild shrubs.

"You hit?" I asked her quickly.

"No—what happened?"

"Shooting at your legs," I told her. That meant at least one of the rifles I'd seen below was a long-range target weapon. In the hands of a marksman good enough to be sure his bullet wouldn't kill her. Dead she couldn't answer questions. With a torn or broken leg she could. He was aiming to knock her down, and his next shot would be for the center of my back.

That ruled out getting up to run again. Which meant we couldn't make it over the hill ahead of our pursuers. But that didn't rule out going *through* the hill. It was for that eventuality that I'd told Christine to bring the flashlight.

"Stay low and close," I told her—and angled up to the left on my hands and knees, keeping to the cover of dense scrub brush. She crawled behind me with her lowered head almost touching my heels.

The bushes didn't make us invisible. They did screen us enough to make us indistinct targets. As long as we stayed low the marksmen couldn't fire again without the risk of hitting Christine with a lethal shot.

The drawback was that crawling was slow. And the pursuit wouldn't be slow. They'd catch up and come at us from four different directions at once before we could get far.

But my objective wasn't that much farther.

When you can't run fast enough to escape from the enemy, the only alternative is to stand and fight. Like it or not. Against five-to-one odds your only chance is to pick the right terrain to make your stand. Preferably a place you know better than they do.

The abandoned central structure of Fort de la Revère was close above us, but we still couldn't see any of it. That was because most of it was sunk into the hilltop, showing only a low profile above ground. I remembered the moat that surrounded it. Deep and wide. A single narrow bridge across it. Leading to the fort's entrance—blocked off now by a big iron door you couldn't break through with anything less than a heavy charge of explosives.

But there were other ways to get inside the fort.

At least there had been—the last time I'd been there.

In the land just ahead of us there was an artificial hump covered by high brush. Going belly-flat I motioned for Christine to do the same. Then I snaked through the bushes, up over the hump. There was a man-made trench with sloped banks below the other side. About six feet wide and seven feet deep. I slid down the near bank to the bottom. It was filled with weeds. They were hip high when I rose in a crouch with my Beretta pistol ready in my fist.

The hump protected us from the opposition, however close they might be by now. How much longer it would continue to do so was the question.

Christine came to her feet beside me. I gestured and we moved off, following the trench to the left. That was the correct direction, if my memory was accurate. It had been a lot of years since I'd last been up here. . . .

Christine was glancing at me anxiously. Not speaking, but her expression said enough. She was as aware as I was of how exposed we were in this trench. No place to hide if they came up over the hump while we were still inside it. My pistol wouldn't be enough against all their weapons. And there was no point in giving her the other pistol. She couldn't handle one with sufficient skill to hit any of the opposition quickly enough.

I pushed on faster through the high weeds. I didn't relish the thought of becoming fertilizer for them.

Seconds later we found what I was looking for. A squared-off hole dug into the base of the trench's right-hand bank. More weeds grew out of its masonry sides, almost concealing the six concrete steps leading down to a low doorway.

One of the underground complex's sally ports—constructed
to allow defense troops to slip out of the fort and mount a
surprise strike against the rear of an attacking force.

The doorway was blocked by an iron-barred gate. Decades of rust had eaten into its bars, but the chain and padlock securing it shut were fairly new. I told Christine to get
over to the opposite bank. She did it quickly, without asking
why. I went down the steps into the confined space of the
sally port and took point-blank aim with the Beretta.

It took two shots to break the padlock open. The first slug
deflected off the lock and vanished into the tunnel behind the
rusted bars. The second ricocheted off a side wall and spun
upward past the back of my neck. I called for Christine while
I unwound the chain from the gate.

She hurried down the steps as I pulled the gate open. I
held out a hand. Christine looked into the dark tunnel and
gave me the flashlight. One thing about her, she didn't need
a lot of explanations. Life had taught her to figure most things
out for herself.

I thumbed on the flashlight and we entered the tunnel.

Wherever Huang and his gang were they would have heard
my shots and my call to Christine. That was fine with me. I
wanted them to find where we'd gone. Some of them would
come in after us. It would be even better if they all did,
concentrating themselves in the narrow route behind us. But
I didn't expect any of it to get that simple. Never plan on the
opposition making dumb moves.

Some would follow us and the rest would spread out to
find other ways in. Their splitting up like that would make it
harder for me in some ways. But it offered certain advantages, too.

The tunnel was high enough for me to stand upright and
wide enough for the two of us to walk side by side. Its concrete walls gleamed wetly in the flashlight's beam. Seepage
of rainwater through the hill above. Little chunks of mortar

had dropped from the ceiling. We crunched them underfoot with every step. The noise carried through the tunnel.

These fortifications, built by France between the World Wars, were all planned along much the same lines. Set into hilltops. With gunports, observation posts, and machine-gun emplacements partially exposed to cover approaches along the slopes. Everything else below ground—ammunition magazines, command posts, kitchens, power plant, store-rooms, communications systems, hospital, and troop quarters. The barracks buildings outside had been for peacetime comfort. When war loomed, everyone was supposed to be garrisoned inside the underground complex.

Which had made for what military planners of the time considered an impregnable defense system. The Maginot Line—with its more than four miles of passages buried deep in the earth—had been the most flamboyant example. And had proved as useless when war did come as the smaller ones like Fort de la Revère, with only a few subterranean levels.

The tunnel we followed linked the sally port to a level two stories under the fort. It ended at a short, narrow stairway leading up to a large, bare room. My flashlight showed an array of graffiti—scratched into its walls by the last soldiers stationed at the fort and by trespassers like me over the years since. It was impossible to be sure what the room had been used for. All furnishings had been stripped away, as they had throughout most of the fort. Judging by a couple of tattered lengths of telephone cable still dangling in one corner, I'd always assumed it had been designed as a subcommand post. And for assembling squads or patrols using the sally port.

The room had two more doorways—their doors carted off long ago—that led into other sections of this level. More rubble crunched underfoot as I led Christine toward one of them. That condition prevailed everywhere in the fort. The good side of that was we'd be able to hear the enemy's approach at any point. The bad side was that between the rubble and the thick layer of dust on the floors, they'd see clear signs of the route we'd taken.

We were going through the doorway when Christine stopped me with a light touch on my arm and pointed back the way we'd come. I lowered the flashlight and listened. After a moment I heard it, too. A very faint crunching sound, reaching us from a distance.

The enemy was into the tunnel behind us now.

⊠ **34** ⊠

WE MOVED ON, GOING FASTER NOW. I TOOK CHRISTINE through a short concrete passageway. It went past the open end of a huge sunken chamber that must have been for munitions storage. A vertical shaft led up from it into a gun turret and was equipped with a mechanical hoist whose gears were frozen with rust. Beyond that the passageway forked. We took the one leading to our right. It went past dark doorways on both sides. Halfway along this passage I turned us into one of them.

After that we were threading our way through a complicated series of rooms. Most I couldn't identify. A few I could.

There was a reservoir area with huge tanks for storing drinking water pumped up from deep wells. If there was any water now in the tanks, it was from seepage. The pumps had been removed—for use elsewhere or for scrap. Another chamber with big tanks could have been a generator room, but the generator was gone, too.

We cut through what looked like a former troop dormitory, judging by the marks of steel lockers and tiers of metal bunks once fastened to the walls. Around the next corner was a long, wide room with holes in the stone floor that had to mean it had once held shower and toilet facilities. Followed by a passage to what was probably a messroom because the one after that was a kitchen. Nobody had yet gotten around to cutting up the big iron stoves to be carted off.

All along our route there were a variety of doorways and passages to choose from. I leaned hard on memories going back over years in picking the ones I took with Christine. Not easy. The last time I'd been there I had been seventeen.

Several times we stopped to listen for sounds behind us. Twice we heard nothing. Once we did—but they were no closer. The opposition was having its own problem. Having to stop and check the ground at every turn to make sure which way our trail led.

In a passage just beyond the kitchen I stopped at a shaft leading straight up to the next level. A little daylight seeped down to us through it. A rusted iron ladder attached to the wall led up the shaft. It didn't look too secure. But then it hadn't even way back when I'd used it with some teenage friends—and it had held then.

And it held when I tried it now. The rivets fastening it to the wall squealed a little but didn't pull loose. A couple rungs bent under my weight but didn't break. I shifted off the top rung onto the concrete floor of the room above, shone the flashlight on my gun hand, and motioned upward. Christine came up faster than I had.

When she was with me, I snicked off the flashlight and put it in my pocket. We didn't need it up on that level, just under the fort's courtyard. There were two small portholes in one wall, high up where it met the ceiling. Enough dim daylight filtered in from them for us to make out everything in the room.

One thing it showed was a pleasant surprise. Lying on the floor was a rusted wire-mesh grill that had fallen from one of the portholes. Apparently nobody had considered that worth carrying off as a souvenir.

It was big enough to partially cover the top of the shaft. Handy for making things just a bit more difficult for the enemy. Every little extra would help.

The dim light in the room also showed a passage leading out of it on this level. But this was as far as I wanted Christine to go.

I took her over to a corner of the room and had her sit down on the floor. With the angle of two walls protecting her back and sides, and her knees up. I got out my spare pistol, the H&K P7, and snicked the safety off before giving it to Christine.

"I'm not a good shot," she whispered.

"You won't have to be," I whispered back quickly. I showed her how to hold the pistol. With both hands, braced on her raised knees. I aimed it for her, tilting the gun to point at the top of the shaft. "Slide your finger across the trigger but don't apply any pressure. It's ready to fire. When you have to, don't *pull* the trigger. Just squeeze gently. And try to hold it steady, aimed at that shaft. They have to come up the ladder one at a time. I'll pull that grill across the top of the shaft when I go down. You see anybody try to move it out of the way, you shoot at it."

"You're leaving me," Christine whispered. It wasn't meant as a question and she didn't seem surprised or accusing. Just stating a fact. And accepting it.

"I'll be back," I told her.

"All right," she said. Accepting that, too, as fact.

"Anytime that grill moves, you start shooting at it," I repeated. "And shout at them. I don't care what you shout. Just make it loud and long so they know it's you up here."

Christine nodded once and concentrated on keeping the pistol aimed at the shaft. Whoever came up it first would have to duck back down when she began shooting. And he wouldn't try blind-firing into the room because any unaimed shot might kill her.

I didn't expect them to stay pinned down in the shaft too long. Given time to think it over, they would split up again. One staying below the shaft to make sure she didn't slip out that way. The other or others circling away to look for some way to get to her from a different direction.

There *were* other ways to reach this room. For that matter, the rest of Huang's men—the ones who by now would have found other entrances into the fort—could chance on her from one of those other directions. But by my reckoning the time element was still in our favor.

I gripped Christine's shoulder gently and briefly before moving back near the top of the shaft. There I paused and listened. No sound below. I got the grill and put it down over part of the shaft opening. Then I went down the ladder. When my head was below the grill, I reached up and pulled it across to cover as much of the opening as it could. Enough so no one could climb up any farther without moving it out of the way.

At the bottom of the shaft I stopped again to listen and look. There was no sound, no glimmer of an approaching flashlight. I took out my own flashlight, aiming it downward in my left hand with my fingers partially screening its lens. Holding the Beretta leveled in my right hand, I thumbed on the light. And went back along the exact route we'd used in the other direction. Carefully. Not shuffling my feet—picking them up and putting them down.

Unless Huang had an eagle-eyed Apache scout among his crew, none of them would spot where I'd backtracked.

The distance between me and the one following our trail was closing fast now. But I got to where I wanted before they did. In the garrison kitchen. Beside a big iron oven that had its lid wide open. I switched off my light and put it in my pocket. Then I climbed into the oven.

I wasn't going to come out of there squeaky clean. But dirty is better than dead.

In the sudden total darkness I felt for the edge of the oven's lid with my free hand. I found it and got set to give it a swift, hard pull. Those hinges were going to let out a rusty screech. Better not to make it a prolonged one.

I yanked the lid almost shut. The rusty screech was short—and loud. They would have heard that. But I doubted they'd be able to identify what it had been. I sat inside the oven and waited, the Beretta trained on the lid and one eye squinting at the darkness outside the two-inch opening I'd left. I didn't think they'd start opening all the ovens for a look inside because they'd be following our trail. But if they did, at least one of them was going to get shot in the face at a range of about four inches.

I waited.

I didn't hear their approach. The iron surrounding me blocked out that kind of sound. First I saw the beam of a flashlight probe into the room. It wasn't until the man holding it entered the room that I heard the crunch of mortar fragments under his shoes.

I couldn't see him in detail. Just a medium-size dark shape. And the glint of light reflected by his weapons. A rifle hanging across his back by a shoulder sling. A long-barreled revolver in the hand not holding the flashlight.

He played the light around the room. It blinded me for a split second before passing on across the other ovens. Then he beamed the light on the floor again and moved across the room, away from me, following the trail Christine and I had left.

One man. All alone. I didn't let that make me too cheerful. Holding myself absolutely still, I watched him halt when he reached the passage we'd taken. He peered into it, using his light. Then he turned his head and motioned with the revolver.

I heard a second man enter the room. When he crossed my line of sight, I saw he was carrying the Uzi.

There was a moment, when he joined the first one, that I could have thrown open the oven and shot them both. But the way they'd entered the room had a professional patience to it that bothered me. The lead man taking time to scout the route before the second showed himself. There could be a third man bringing up the rear and delaying his appearance the way the second had. There could even be a fourth and fifth. . . .

By the time I was sure there were only these two, they were gone—vanished into the passage leading to the shaft. And that opportunity was gone with them.

I waited again. Not mad at myself for having held back. Because it had been the correct combat procedure under the circumstances—even if the precaution had proved needless.

I stayed inside my oven and listened. My free hand against the inside of the lid but not pushing it open. The noise it would make again—sounding *behind* them—would bring them back on the double with their weapons ready. Climbing out with that submachine gun spitting large quantities of lead at me wouldn't earn me anything. Not even a Silver Star on my grave. Not even a decent burial.

So—I waited.

The bark of pistol shots echoed loudly down the passage from the direction of the shaft. Three of them—followed by Christine screaming something prolonged in a language I didn't understand. What I did register was that it didn't sound forced. It sounded wild—as though she were out of control.

By the time the racket of the shooting and screaming ended, it had served to cover the short protest of the oven lid when I shoved it wide open.

I climbed out and hunkered down beside the ovens. Back to waiting. Taking slow, shallow breaths of air.

When she started shooting and yelling again, I crossed the room and moved into the passage.

⊠ **35** ⊠

I LEFT THE FLASHLIGHT IN MY POCKET AND FELT MY WAY out of the dark kitchen with my outstretched free hand. Once I was into the passage, the faint daylight filtering down out of the shaft up ahead showed me the way. It also showed me one of the opposition. He stood under the bottom of the shaft, looking up. I could make out the rifle across his back and the revolver in his hand.

The one with the Uzi submachine gun was up inside the shaft. Where I couldn't see him.

I raised the Beretta and took careful aim at the man I could see. But I didn't want to shoot until I was closer and could see them both. Holding my aim, I moved toward my target. Staying close to one wall of the passage. Taking one long, careful step at a time. Testing each step, quietly moving rubble away with my foot before putting my weight on it.

I stopped when I was close enough but not too close. Any closer and the light from the shaft would reach me. The position was as good as it was going to get where I was. I still blended into the darkness of the passage wall. The opposition would be in the light. The difference in visibility compensated for their two-to-one superiority.

I could see the feet of the one in the shaft now. He was coming down. Carefully feeling for each rung. I didn't want to have to shoot them both. Not if I could control what hap-

pened next and buy a chance to question one about where
the others were. But whether I could exercise that kind of
control was up to them more than me. In a kill-or-be-killed
situation, survival is the overriding factor.

Most of the guy in the shaft came into view. He was carrying the Uzi in one hand, using his other hand to grip the
ladder rungs. His feet were on the third rung from the bottom
when I snapped out the order: "Freeze and drop your guns—
don't turn around!"

They didn't freeze.

The one below the shaft spun with his revolver toward the
sound of my voice. A stupid move because he had to search
for me and I had never shifted aim away from him. My bullet
hammered into his temple and knocked him over into the
dark beyond the shaft.

The other one had jumped off the ladder, twisting around
as he dropped with the Uzi firing a long burst in my direction. The slugs lashed past and thudded off the passage walls
behind me. But in that confined a space against a weapon
that sprays six hundred rounds per minute you don't count
on the bullets continuing to avoid you for long. I shot him
three times as he landed on his feet. The first shot kicked
him in the stomach and doubled him over. The next two
smashed into his chest and drove him back half a step before
his legs buckled and he fell forward on his face.

I reached him quickly. No life signs. Taking out my flashlight, I switched it on as I stepped past him into the darkness
where the other lay. Assuming a head shot is automatically
a kill is a mistake you don't make after you've been through
a lot of combat. I've seen men survive incredible head
wounds.

The one I'd hit in the temple wasn't one of them. The
revolver lay beside his inert hand. I picked it up. A Manurhin
.357 Magnum, fully loaded. I stuck it in my belt. The more
firepower the better.

His rifle was still across his back. A lever-action Browning

B-92. A good weapon but not for long-range marksmanship. The man who'd shot at Christine's legs was elsewhere in or around the fort.

Wherever the others were they would have heard the shooting in here. But the way sounds echoed through the subsurface levels they wouldn't be able to judge exactly where the sound had come from. Unless they were very close. I stood still and listened. Nothing.

Putting the flashlight away, I returned to the man with the Uzi. There was a spare ammo clip sticking out of one of his pockets. I removed the partially used clip and snapped in the new one. The one I'd removed had some rounds left. I stuck it in my pocket, holstered my Beretta, and kept the Uzi in hand when I went up the ladder. The odds had been cut by two but that left three. A submachine gun would be more useful than a pistol against that number.

Pausing just below the grill I called softly, "Christine— it's me. Sawyer. You're—"

I didn't get to finish it because she fired two shots at the top of the shaft. One of them spanged off the grill and moved it a few inches. I ducked lower and listened to her yelling again. I still couldn't make out what she was saying. She'd reverted to Vietnamese.

When she stopped, I tried again: "It's all right now, Christine . . ."

I heard several distinctive clicks up there. She was trying to fire again, but the pistol I'd given her was now empty. I pushed the grill aside and climbed out of the shaft.

Christine was huddled in the corner the way I'd left her, with the H&K braced on her raised knees. What was different was her dazed expression. I took out the flashlight and shined it on my face. "It's me, Christine," I told her quietly.

After a moment she opened her hands. The pistol slid down her shins and came to rest on the floor by her feet. She straightened a bit, shaking her head like someone having trouble waking up. I put away the flashlight and held my hand out to her. Christine grasped it with both of hers and let me help her to her feet.

For a moment she sagged against me. Then she stiffened herself and moved back a step. "I'm . . . sorry." Her voice was low and dead flat. "My mind—slipped. I thought . . ."

She didn't finish it and didn't have to. What had happened to her was obvious. For a few minutes she'd been back on that refugee boat with the pirates climbing aboard. The circumstances were similar enough. Both the danger and the kind of men it came from.

"Did you kill them?" she asked in that same dead-flat tone.

"Two of them."

"Good."

She picked up the empty pistol and gave it to me. I stuffed it in the pocket with the binoculars. I was beginning to feel like a walking arsenal. "We've got to move now," I said. "Can you manage?"

She nodded. The dazed look was going. With my finger across the Uzi's trigger I led the way into a corridor angling out of the room. Christine followed without a word. She wasn't someone bubbling over with faith in mankind, but ever since she'd made the decision to come with me her trust had been total. I didn't know what she'd seen or sensed in me to cause that. But I understood the depth of the compliment it implied. And the responsibility that went with it.

I was grateful she didn't ask me to explain where we were going because I couldn't be sure I was doing the right thing.

Even if you make all the right moves, luck influences the outcome. Some of the best soldiers I'd known were gone because they'd run into the bad variety. A rescue chopper malfunctioning in midair. A land mine where nobody logical would have planted one. Even the gods and demons, some-one said way back when they believed in gods and demons, are helpless against luck. Both varieties.

Bad luck had been Huang arriving when he did. Twenty minutes later we would have been gone. Since then, we'd run to a streak of good luck. No way to know how long that would hold or if it was about to turn on us.

One thing sure. If we and the enemy kept wandering around in this claustrophobic complex, we were bound to run into one another eventually. They could be around the next corner. They were down from five to three, and I had the Uzi. But that still didn't make for an evenly matched fight.

We had two choices. We could try to slip out of the fort and down the other slopes where we'd have a good chance of losing the opposition. Or we could pick a place to hide inside the fort until night—depending on their not finding us before darkness came and helped us to get away.

The losing history of these forts built for a passive defense—and my own instincts—argued against just pulling inside a shell and hoping for the best through the long hours that would follow. I opted for making the try now.

One factor was in favor of that. At least one of them, and perhaps all three, would be *inside* the fort—searching for the source of the gunfire between us and the two who'd been eliminated. That should make the slopes outside the fort partly or entirely clear for a while.

We got to a narrow stairwell that took us back down to the lowest level. I listened for a time before using the flashlight. Nobody between us and the next corner. I gave Christine the light. She followed a step behind, shining it past me, keeping the beam low. When we reached the next corner, I went into a low crouch and gestured behind me. Christine switched off the light.

Staying crouched, I turned the corner with the Uzi leading the way. Nothing happened. I listened for a few seconds and then felt Christine coming around beside me, crouched as low as I was. She learned fast. I tapped her forearm. She snicked the light on and quickly swung its beam around the large, stripped-bare room we'd entered. Nobody there but us.

I straightened and walked to a big round hole in the stone floor.

When it rained in these mountains, it came down hard. The underground levels would have filled with water except for a lot of strategically placed storm drains like this one. All of them had once been covered with heavy iron gratings. But those had been sold to scrapyards after the place had been abandoned.

The entire drainage system had been made extralarge to insure that water wouldn't back up and knock out the fort's electricity. During World War II—when the Axis had used the place to hold captured Allied airmen—a number of prisoners had used this system to escape. Investigating the escape routes had been one of the first things we'd done when I'd come up there with other kids to explore.

I had brought Christine to this particular drain shaft because it led to the shortest route out beyond the front of the fort. And the slopes out there had the most cover. I was hunkered down beside the open hole, listening, when Christine joined me. It was unlikely that any of the enemy would have been waiting down there all this time on the chance we'd use this route. But unlikely didn't mean impossible. I took the light from Christine, switched it off, stuck it in a pocket.

In utter darkness I hung the Uzi over my shoulder by its sling.

"Wait here," I whispered in Christine's ear. I felt the edge of the hole, gripped it with both hands, and lowered myself into black emptiness.

The depth of this drain shaft, I knew from the past, was almost exactly eleven feet. During our youthful explorations we'd brought rope along. I didn't have any rope now. But I was taller than I'd been then. When I was hanging full-length, the soles of my shoes were only some three feet from the bottom. I let go and dropped. Spreading my feet apart and bending my knees to cushion the impact.

The instant I landed I ripped the Uzi from my shoulder. But nobody fired at me. I got the flashlight and turned it on.

I was inside a wide cave. This area was honeycombed with natural pockets. Wherever possible the engineers had used them as part of the drainage system. A big runoff pipe led into one side of the cave. Another led out of it. Most of the uneven stone floor was covered by a thick layer of mud. It was springy-hard after more than three weeks without rain.

I laid the Uzi on the hard mud and put the flashlight down beside it with the beam shining upward. Raising both hands above my head, I signaled to Christine. Her dim figure came into view above, hung down by her hands, then let go and dropped. I caught her in my arms. Lowering her until she was standing, I picked up the Uzi and gave her the flashlight.

We crossed the cave and entered the runoff pipe to our right. I had to crouch to get in, but Christine could stand almost upright. When we were both inside it, I had her switch off the light and put it in her pocket. It was impossible to see an inch ahead after that. Christine held onto the back of my jacket and I felt my way through the pipe, trailing one hand along the top of it.

After some twenty steps we came to a big opening above us. The bottom of another drain shaft. I stopped to listen for sounds above before moving on. I did the same at others we passed under. And at each of two side runoff pipes that joined the one we were in. After we passed the second of those, I knew we were below the courtyard buildings constructed against the inner face of the fort's main wall, near its single entrance.

A few steps farther I saw daylight ahead. Coming from where the storm drain ended. The moat.

I reached the end of the pipe and went down on one knee, looking out. I knew the proportions of the moat by heart. Eighteen feet wide and almost thirty feet deep. Its inner and outer walls lined with large blocks of stone. I couldn't see much of it from inside the pipe. Only some of the lower part of the outer wall directly across the moat from me. And— six feet below the end of my pipe—the moat's bottom, covered with low bushes and ground-creeping vines.

Leaning my head out just enough, I looked swiftly to the left and right. Scanning first the top of the moat's outer wall. Nobody was in sight anywhere along it. Nor on the bridge, forty yards to my right, which crossed the moat from its outer wall to the iron door blocking the fort's entrance.

The moat was empty, too—as far as I could see to where the front of the fort cornered to my left and right. The weeds in the bottom of the moat were dense, but not high enough to conceal anyone.

What I couldn't see from my vantage point was the top of the inner moat wall and the fort's main wall above me. I jumped from the pipe into the bottom of the moat. The noise of bushes crushed under me was very loud in the silence around the fort. And the noise continued as I strode to the middle of the moat, breaking branches and vines that entangled my legs.

I spun to a halt, scanning the front wall of the fort above me with the Uzi held ready for rapid fire. There was no one up there. In either direction.

Dragging a deep breath, I looked toward my objective. It was less than ten yards away, between me and the bridge. A big opening in the bottom of the moat's outer wall. The mouth of a drain that led to the slopes beyond and below the fort. Our escape route.

Christine was crouched inside the pipe we'd come through. I waved to her. She jumped down into the moat and began wading through the dense weeds toward me.

That was when our luck turned sour.

⊠ 36 ⊠

I CAUGHT A FLASH OF MOVEMENT ABOVE THE MOAT AND twisted in its direction. A man had appeared atop the moat's outer wall near the bridge.

Huang.

He had a handgun. He was gripping it with both hands and bringing it around to aim down at me. But the range was too far for accuracy with a handgun.

I brought the Uzi up to bear on him. It was too far for accuracy with that, too. But a submachine gun has a psychological plus factor. It scares hell out of anybody at the wrong end of it. Huang leaped back out of sight before either of us could fire.

An instant after he vanished, there were two rapid shots from his handgun. It had to be a signal—summoning the forces he had left. From inside or outside the fort. Or inside *and* outside. Wherever the other two were, they would be converging on this area.

There were other exit drains from the moat. Far away around the other sides of the fort. But the entangling weeds made it impossible to run any distance fast enough. We would be exposed in the bottom of the moat too long. Easy targets— for the shotgun and especially for that marksman's rifle.

I charged through the brush toward the nearest and fastest exit. The big drain under the outer wall less than ten yards away. When I got there, I put my back to the wall beside it, aiming the Uzi upward. Christine reached me seconds later.

"In," I rasped.

She went in and I was turning to go after her when one of Huang's men appeared inside the fort. It was the one with the shotgun. He was atop the wall across the moat from me. On a narrow walkway that cut behind the big iron door sealing the fort entrance off from the bridge.

It wasn't a good range for either his shotgun or my Uzi— but he tried. The shotgun boomed and pellets spattered against the wall above the exit drain as I dodged inside.

I caught up with Christine and sprinted past her. It was fast going in there. The big drainpipe inclined downward. It was bottomed with hard mud and the weeds growing out of it weren't thick enough to impede us.

The three of them would be converging on the area where we'd be coming out of the pipe. Huang, the shotgunner, and the marksman with the rifle.

I was under no illusion that the big iron entrance door would prevent the shotgunner from getting out of the fort and across the moat. Anyone of reasonable agility could climb *around* the door onto the bridge. I'd done it often enough myself.

Huang worried me least. Even at close quarters. I liked the odds of my Uzi against his handgun as much as he would dislike it.

The marksman worried me most. I didn't know the direction and distance of his approach route.

I stopped—and stopped Christine behind me—when I reached the end of the storm drain. The water that poured out of it during rains had cut a deep, wide gully down the slopes below it. A dense woods rare for this area filled the gully and spread wide over both banks. The trees were stumpy and wind-twisted. Few were taller than four feet. Their branches spread out rather than up, with their foliage hanging close over the ground. Protected by the trees, underbrush grew profuse and high. In many places the under-brush and tree foliage met and mingled.

Perfect stalking cover. Reason enough for my having chosen this route.

I pulled Christine close beside me while I kept watch on the gully and flanking woodland outside.

"Give me a few minutes out there to grab all their attention," I whispered quickly. "Then go back the way we came. They'll think you went out after me while they were concentrating on me. Cross the moat and climb back into the pipe we came out of. Turn into the first side pipe you get to. Hide there until I come calling for you. If I don't come, stay hidden there until night and . . ."

But Christine was shaking her head. "No. I have to get back to our place and warn Marc. They'll go there if they can't find me."

"You're no use to your boyfriend if you don't survive," I growled. "That comes first."

"No," she repeated. Softly—but with no give in it at all.

Love always complicates things.

And I didn't have any time left to waste on arguing against it. "At least stay put in here until I get back. All right?"

She nodded. Just once. I pushed her behind me, deeper inside the storm drain, and gave all my attention to my own survival problem.

Huang and the shotgunner would be coming from the direction of the bridge. Therefore toward the gully's right bank. But they wouldn't have reached it yet. The shotgunner because it would take a bit longer to get here from where he'd started. Huang because he wouldn't come until the shotgunner joined him.

He wouldn't come alone. Not because he was a coward. Huang had probably begun his career as a thug with a gun. But he was a big businessman now. Accustomed to having underlings handle the dirty job, according to his directions, while he stood back waiting for results. I'd seen his performance at the wharf in Antwerp.

So I had a few more minutes before I had to cope with Huang and the shotgunner.

What about the third man—with the marksman's rifle?

Assume the worst. He was already here, watching my exit route. A careful crawl out of my shelter would only give him more time to get a bead on me.

Okay—that's the condition that prevails. Now deal with it.

I launched myself out into the gully on the jump. Hunched forward to make myself as small a moving target as possible. Angling up the right bank through heavy brush under low-spreading trees. On the third jump I reversed direction and dived for the bottom of the gully.

A shot ripped foliage at the top of the right bank. Where I would have been if I hadn't changed course.

A rifle shot.

I crashed down into a pack of high bushes curled in a tight ball and did a fast roll under a gnarled kermes oak. Went flat and squirmed under a dense growth of juniper. Bumped into the thick base of a scrub holm and slithered around it as the rifle blasted again. The bullet thunked into dirt a good foot behind me.

A long-barreled target rifle is great where you have space to swing it. But shifting aim with it quickly is difficult inside dense cover. And the marksman using it was either lazy or not used to shooting at targets that might shoot back. He wasn't moving around enough. His second shot had come from the same area as his first—somewhere up along the gully's left bank.

Keeping the thick low trunk of the holm between me and his approximate position, I dug the binoculars out of my pocket. I tossed them underhand at a target a few feet away from me, making sure its flight would be hidden by overhanging foliage all the way. It dropped into a thick clump of evergreen shrubs, rustling them noisily. A third rifle shot tore into the shrubs there and chopped up a gout of dry dirt and dust.

He was up near the top of the left bank, somewhere between a stunted beech tree and a maritime pine. I tilted the Uzi and squeezed the trigger, lashing the area between the pine and the beech on full automatic, aiming low. The stubby submachine gun shuddered in my hands as I kept raking long bursts back and forth, the bullets shredding foliage and chopping out chunks of splintered wood.

The ammo clip emptied itself. I was doing a fast job of disengaging it when the marksman came tumbling down the left bank, rolling over and over. He'd left his rifle behind. He was no longer concerned about it. Or any other possessions. You can't take them with you.

I snapped the other clip into the Uzi. It was partly used but had half of its rounds left. I scuttled down the gully, keeping under cover all the way. Then I swung over the right bank and began working up behind it, circling wide through the thick, low woods. Huang and his shotgunner were due there about now.

When I reckoned I was high enough, I went to the ground. Snaking forward on my elbows and toes, angling back toward the top of the right bank. Under low-hanging trees. Between rocks. Through high weeds. I stopped to look and listen carefully. Then moved on. Stopped to look and listen again. Moved on. Stopped.

Huang stood on top of the right bank, partially hidden under the shadow of a scrub oak. He was holding the handgun—a compact automatic. But he didn't look ready to use it. Unless an easy target he couldn't resist happened to show itself. He was peering down the right bank at a nearby grove of low pines.

That would be where the shotgunner had taken his position.

I snaked toward Huang between high patches of lentisk shrubs. When I was close enough, with a low outcrop of rock between me and the shotgunner's position, I came up on one knee and said softly, "Huang . . ."

He turned toward me very slowly. Lowering the automatic before he completed the turn. He looked at me and he looked at the Uzi trained on him. His expression was wooden. He opened his hand and let the automatic fall to the ground.

"Call your man with the shotgun," I said just loud enough for him to hear. "Have him come up here."

Huang nodded. A practical man agreeing to a request he considered reasonable under the circumstances. He turned his head and looked down at the grove of pines again and called out a name I didn't get.

There was no response from the grove.

Huang got a faintly irritated look. He called out again, louder: "Come back up here. I want you—now."

There was a gunshot in the grove down there.

Not the heavy thump of a shotgun. The sharp crack of a handgun. Followed quickly by another.

The shotgunner came into sight out of the trees. Moving slowly, uncertainly. As he took his second step the shotgun spilled from his hands. On the next step his legs turned to rubber. He toppled forward on his face and didn't move again.

⊠ 37 ⊠

HUANG WAS STARING DOWN AT THE NEARBY PINE GROVE. His mouth hung partly open but his expression wasn't a puzzled one. Neither of us had much doubt about what had happened in that grove. Nor about who had made it happen.

There was a movement in the foliage at the edge of the grove near where the shotgunner lay. And a few moments later another movement, higher on the slope and nearer to us. He was coming up. Sticking to cover all the way.

I moved closer to the protection of the rock outcrop and waited with the Uzi. But when he stepped into view, it was from an unexpected direction. On the other side of Huang.

The gun in his hand was the large revolver I'd seen tucked in his belt when we'd met aboard that barge in Antwerp. He faced Huang with that scary smile.

I shifted the Uzi to cover him but Huang was between us, spreading his empty hands wide and saying, "I'm not armed, Colin."

"So I see," Colin said, and shot him twice in the chest.

The impact spun Huang against the scrub oak. He leaned against it looking emptily at Colin. He went on staring after he slid to the ground in a sitting position and his head tipped back against the tree trunk. The stare was no longer directed at Colin. It was merely the expression he'd had on his face before his heart stopped ticking.

209

"I would have always had to worry about you finding me," Colin said to the dead man. "I'm at a point in life where I'm tired of problems."

I was on my feet by then with the Uzi pointing at him. Colin had the revolver pointed at me. I said, "You shoot that and it won't kill me fast enough to stop me squeezing this trigger and tearing you apart."

"I don't have any reason to shoot you," he said lightly. "Unless you try something fancy. And I know you don't want to kill *me*. I'm the only one can get our lady lawyer out of trouble."

Standoff. I wished it weren't the Uzi I was holding on him now. With a pistol I could have broken his gun arm with a fast shot. But a submachine gun on full automatic can't be controlled that minutely. And he was right—I didn't want to kill him.

"You followed Huang here," I said.

"Sure. I've been following him all the time. Ever since Antwerp." Colin smiled that smile. "I *told* you I might find her first."

Without looking away from me he yelled out: "Christine! It's me—Dédé! It's safe out here now!"

"Don't come out!" I called to her. "Stay where you are!"

But she didn't.

I heard her climbing up the slope. After a while I glimpsed her out of the corner of my eye. She stopped when she saw Colin standing there holding the revolver. Then she continued coming.

My finger tensed across the Uzi's trigger. I *didn't* want to kill Colin—but I was going to if he turned that revolver on her.

All he turned was his head. Just enough to see her when she was near us. His smile when he looked at her was entirely different from any I'd seen on him before. There was nothing scary in it.

He said, "Hello, my love—I've been looking for you."

"And I've been waiting for you, Dédé," she said with an odd smile of her own.

I snapped at her, "Don't get between us."

But she did. She moved between us to Colin. She raised her left hand to grasp the nape of his neck and came up on her toes as though she wanted to kiss him. Her right hand was between them and I couldn't see what it was doing.

He was smiling down at her when he said, "I hope you still have that rabbit."

And then he wasn't smiling. He staggered back a step and his expression was one of utter astonishment—and then pain.

Christine stepped away from him. The hilt of the knife she'd drawn from her belt sheath protruded from him, a little below the breastbone. Just the hilt. All of the blade was deep inside him.

He still held the revolver but he didn't try to bring it to bear on Christine. Just stared at her—and then down at the knife that had become part of him. He sagged to his knees still looking at it. Then slowly fell over on his side and rolled on his back.

I walked to him and went down on one knee, carefully removing the gun from his hand. There was no resistance in his fingers. His lips were drawn back in a grimace of agony. Blood began to bubble through his clenched teeth.

I asked him quickly, "Who gave you the gun you used when you escaped from prison?"

He tried to grin at me but he couldn't manage it. "Go to hell," he whispered through his clenched, bloody teeth.

"You can tell them to expect me," I said, but Colin was on his way before I finished it.

I stood up and asked Christine, "What is the rabbit he was talking about?"

She didn't seem to hear. She was looking at Colin. With a numbed, leaden expression. Perhaps the way she had looked at the injured baby who'd died in her arms on that looted refugee boat in the Gulf of Thailand when she was thirteen.

I repeated the question.

This time she told me the answer.

I NURSED A GLASS OF ROSÉ AT A SIDEWALK TABLE OF A BRAS-
serie terrace on the Champs-Élysées. Not my favorite street
in Paris, as I may have mentioned. The office building next
door contained the headquarters of the richest and most in-
fluential of the companies that had insured the jewelry stolen
at Antibes. On the chair beside me sat a gray and brown
stuffed rabbit no bigger than my hand.

It was shabby and discolored from years of tight hugging
and unavoidable battering. The cloth loop by which a child
could carry it was torn. Much of its face had been worn away.
One ear was entirely gone. Christine Boyer had lost everything she had from the past several times during her young
life. This was all she'd managed to save through all those
losses. Her mother had given her the stuffed rabbit before
she was old enough to speak—and had always told her it was
a present from the father she hadn't known.

It was the one object she had never let go of. She had
carried it with her from Vietnam to Thailand. To France and
Antwerp and back to France.

Colin hadn't allowed Christine to get her things from her
apartment when he'd been waiting outside the Bangkok Bar
to take her away. But he had already broken into the apartment and taken the stuffed rabbit. He'd had it waiting for her
in his car.

He knew it was the one thing she would never, under any circumstances, leave behind.

I was finishing my rosé when Arlette Alfani came out of the building next door. She was followed by a plump, balding man with a soft face set into a permanent look of trustworthy dignity. He wore the requisite professional costume. Exquisitely tailored black three-piece suit and silver-gray silk necktie. Serious. Dependable. At the moment a bit anxious.

Arlette introduced him to me as Monsieur Despont, director of the insurance company. The other firms that had insured various pieces of the stolen jewelry had agreed to have him represent them all.

I cleared the chair next to me, setting the stuffed rabbit on my lap. Arlette sat down and I gestured for Despont to take another chair. He preferred to continue standing. He was too well trained to shuffle from foot to foot, but he stood there waiting with barely controlled impatience.

"Did you get what you need?" I asked Arlette. She nodded and I said I'd like to see it. Arlette took a folded letter from an envelope and gave it to me. I unfolded it and read carefully.

It was from the Ministry of the Interior. It stated that Arlette Alfani had been cleared of any suspicion of complicity regarding the escape of André Colin from prison—in gratitude for her assistance to the government in obtaining the return of the jewelry stolen by Colin and unknown others from guests at the party in Antibes.

"You will note," Monsieur Despont pointed out to me needlessly and firmly, "that the continuing validity of that letter depends entirely on our *getting* the jewelry back."

"The jewelry," I told him, "is in the vault of the Banque de France branch on Place Clichy. In a safe-deposit box André Colin rented there and paid for five years in advance."

I dug into the belly of the stuffed rabbit through the seam that Christine Boyer had delicately unstitched at my request. I still wondered when Colin had done his own delicate job of unstitching and restitching it. In Antwerp? Or after they were in Paris? Christine had no idea. She'd never known about Colin using her rabbit as his hiding place.

I found one of the two hidden items inside the stuffing. A document folded many times to form a tight square. I gave it to Despont. "From the bank—Colin's authorization to use that safe-deposit." I felt through the stuffing again. "And the key to the box." I put it on the table.

Despont had unfolded the bank document and was reading it swiftly, beginning to allow himself a slight smile.

"I imagine," I said, "that the bank's manager will co-operate in allowing you to open that box to retrieve the stolen goods."

"I am sure of it," Despont stated. He put the document in his breast pocket. He picked up the key reverently, as though it were a piece of the Holy Grail. "Well—all's well that ends well, eh?"

"I'll have to think about that one," I said, and ignored the kick Arlette delivered to my ankle under the table.

Despont regarded me uncertainly. Then he beamed at Arlette, assured her of his undying gratitude for her assistance, shook her hand, and marched triumphantly back into his building.

I got up and told Arlette, "Let's go home."

I took her hand as she stood up. With my other hand I picked up the stuffed rabbit. "I promised to get this back to Christine quickly. She and her sculptor would like us both to come up to their place and have dinner with them when I do."

"When are they expecting us?"

"Tomorrow. Tonight's just you and me."

"Lovely thought," Arlette said, smiling and linking her fingers through mine. She tightened her grip on my hand as we walked away together.

About the Author

Marvin H. Albert was born in Philadelphia and has lived in New York, Los Angeles, London, Rome, and Paris. He currently lives on the Riviera with his wife, the French artist Xenia Klar. He has two children, Jan and David.

He has been a Merchant Marine Officer, actor and theatrical road manager, newspaperman, magazine editor, and Hollywood scriptwriter, in addition to being the author of numerous books of fiction and non-fiction.

Several of his novels have been Literary Guild choices. He has been honored with a Special Award by the Mystery Writers of America. Nine of his novels have been made into motion pictures.

THE MIDNIGHT SISTER is the sixth book in the *Stone Angel* series.

The Mysterious
MARVIN ALBERT

A truly distinctive mystery series neatly fitting together with interesting plots, rich with suspense.